AN ARTFUL LIE

HOLLY NEWMAN

OLIVER HEBER BOOKS

CHAPTER 1

THE ROYAL ACADEMY OF ART
EXHIBITION

"Bella!"
Lady Isabella Blessingame turned from her study of the large painting *Waterloo: Final Defeat of the French* by George Jones to look about for the source of the voice. She'd heard that the crowds in The Great Room of the Royal Academy of Art had been large every day, though this year's exhibition had been open since late April and it was now June. It would be hard to find anyone in this mass of people that came from all walks of life.

"Bella!" she heard again, then she saw a hand waving at her. She smiled, and despite herself, her eyes watered as memories flooded her mind. Blasted nuisance. They did that at times, her memories, calling forth powerful emotions, try as she might to keep them in the past.

She threaded her way between knots of people to meet the Dowager Duchess of Malmsby. Trust the Duchess to shout at someone across a crowded room. Done by anyone else, it would be considered bad ton —dreadfully vulgar. Lady Malmsby was a force unto herself. She smiled at the memories of spending time with Lady Malmsby and her granddaughters.

Bella hadn't seen the older woman since she'd left the Villa de Fiori two years ago, a little more than a month after her husband, Sir Harry Blessingame, had been killed.

Lord William Candelstone, the Duchess's son-in-law and a spymaster for the crown, had briskly decreed the time for grief was later, when the war with Napoleon was at an end. He'd pressed her into continuing her cryptography work and completing Harry's spy work. Numbly, she'd complied for a year, until the day after the Battle of Waterloo.

At the time of the battle, she'd been in Brussels with many of the international diplomatic denizens who weren't in Vienna. There were spies everywhere, some for Napoleon, some for the Alliance, some for neither side but gathering data for whoever crossed their palms with gold.

Her assignment from Lord Candelstone had been to provide cryptography to captured French communications for Wellington and his generals, and to observe and report on Vizconde Miguel Carrasco-Torres, the Spanish envoy to Brussels, and to Bella's consternation, quite a lecherous man. Unfortunately, as the Spanish envoy, society accepted him everywhere.

Candelstone suspected he was also a spy for Napoleon.

It had proven easy to get into Carrasco-Torres's circle of friends and acquaintances. It had been difficult to keep his hands off her body.

When news of the victory reached Brussels, he'd wanted to celebrate the occasion with her.

Intimately.

She decided her employment with Lord Candelstone had to end—right then. She was not like her late husband, who would jump into bed with any woman —or man—he thought could provide knowledge useful to the war effort! She'd packed up and left the city amidst the fireworks and party celebrations everywhere.

She talked her way onto a packet returning to England and hid for the past year, away from any society, at Lennox Hill, the small property in Derbyshire she'd acquired with her marriage settlement.

However, when she'd learned Lord Candelstone had found out through her brother where she lived and that he wanted her to come back to work for him, and since her solicitors, or more correctly, Harry's solicitors, summoned her to London to give her further information about her inheritance, she would confront Candelstone while in the city. Besides, it was time to return to London and return to society. She vowed she would tell Candelstone face-to-face that there was no way she was going to resume any spy or cryptography activities.

She'd had a long time to think. She considered him responsible for Harry's death. He had known he was sending Harry into a dangerous situation. Harry did, too, but for Harry it was a game. Candelstone did not consider anyone's safety in his plans. He just decreed it was a job that had to be done—for king and country—and he sent off someone to do it.

Lady Malmsby grasped her hands when they met in the center of the Great Room.

"Bella, oh Bella, it is so wonderful to see you!" raved the petite, silver-haired Duchess. She leaned forward and brushed Bella's cheeks on either side with a light kiss in the continental fashion.

"Where have you been? Why no correspondence,

you naughty girl?" Lady Malmsby asked. She tucked one arm around Bella and pulled her to her side. The Duchess then held out her other hand to the woman who had followed her across the large room.

"Sally! Do you know Lady Isabella Blessingame?"

"No, though I have heard you speak of her many times," Lady Sally Oakley said warmly.

"Bella, this is Lady Sally Oakley. She is Lady Travis's sister!"

"Lady Travis from the Villa de Fiori?"

The dowager nodded. "The same. They don't look at all alike, do they?" she said with a chuckle.

"Oh, I don't know," Bella said thoughtfully. "While their coloring is different, their smiles are the same. I always thought Lady Travis had a beautiful smile."

"Bless you, child!" Lady Oakley enthused, her smile radiating. She turned to the Duchess. "Can we keep her?" she asked playfully.

Lady Malmsby laughed. "I should think so." She turned to Bella. "Have you seen my granddaughter, Ann, yet?"

"Ann is here?"

"Yes, in the Red Room with her fiancé."

"Ann is betrothed?"

"My, you have been rusticating," Lady Malmsby said. "Yes, to the Duke of Ellinbourne."

"The Duke of Ellinbourne!"

Lady Malmsby smiled broadly as she nodded. "And Helena is betrothed as well—she, to the Earl of Norwalk."

The melancholy that had gripped Bella since she'd returned to London eased. The news about her friends raised her spirits. They were so good to her and helped her so in the month following Harry's death. "This is wonderful news! And do you approve of the matches?"

"Heartily."

"It's cousins marrying cousins," Lady Oakley said.

"Cousins marrying cousins?" Bella repeated, confused.

"What Sally means is the Earl and the Duke are cousins, as are Ann and Helena," Lady Malmsby explained.

Bella's brow cleared. "Oh. I understand. Is Helena in the city as well?"

"Alas, no," Lady Malmsby said with an exaggerated pout. Then she smiled again to negate the dramatics. "There have been issues at her father's porcelain factory that have needed attention," she explained. "But we shall have a betrothal ball for her and the Earl in the fall after Michaelmas. — And speaking of betrothal balls, Ann and the Duke's betrothal ball is three nights hence. You must give me your direction so we can send you an invitation."

"Right now, as my brother has rooms at the regiment barracks, I am staying at Mivart's Hotel until I can rent us a townhouse to share."

"Who is your brother, dear?" Lady Oakley asked.

"Captain Andrew Melville."

"Really?" Lady Oakley said. She raised her eyebrows as she turned to look at Lady Malmsby.

Bella laughed. "I know we are not alike. He used to work at the Alien Office for Lord Candelstone; however, since that man retired, my brother has felt lost. His is a loyal soul."

"Lady Malmsby told me you worked for Lord Candelstone as well," Lady Oakley observed.

"I did," Bella conceded, "until the day after the

Battle of Waterloo. Napoleon had been defeated, and I just wanted to come home."

"I don't blame you," Lady Malmsby said. "But why have you hidden yourself away?"

Bella felt the pall of melancholy sweep over her again.

"I needed time to mourn," she said simply. "And I needed to decide what I want to do with my life. I'd only been married to Sir Harry Blessingame for nine months when he died, and then I was pitched into the war effort without time to think about Harry or what I would do. I was like a wind-up automaton. Lord Candelstone kept me so busy that there wasn't time to think about the future. We were dealing with the war in the present."

"Well, I, for one, am glad you have decided to re-enter society at last," said Lady Malmsby. "I have a suggestion, and know I will not take *no* for an answer." Lady Malmsby slipped her arm through Bella's and pulled her closer to her side. "Staying at a hotel, no matter the quality of the hotel, is not something a lady should do alone, even if she is a respectable widow," Lady Malmsby told her, her tone quite serious. "You should come to Malmsby House and stay with us until you secure rental lodgings. Malmsby House is commodious, I assure you."

"That is an excellent idea," Lady Oakley agreed.

Bella canted her head. "I'll own, I should like to stay some place not as populous and loud day and night as Mivart's," she slowly said. "But isn't that the Duke's home?" she asked.

"Arthur won't care," Lady Malmsby said airily. "Truthfully, I doubt Arthur would notice. And Lancelot and Guinevere have conveyed to me they have quite enjoyed the activity I have brought to the house."

Bella blinked at the trio of names. "You have an Arthur, a Guinevere and a Lancelot? How could I not know that?"

Lady Malmsby laughed. "I did name my son Arthur; however, it was his poor wife, Morgana, who named the twins after Guinevere and Lancelot, and their last child, Merlin."

"Was she a King Arthur lore enthusiast?" Bella asked.

"Yes, however, it is my son, the Duke, who is the Arthurian scholar. He was always of a bookish bent, and with Arthur as his name and Morgana as his wife's name, I suppose it is not surprising that their children would have Arthurian legend names, even if in legend Lancelot and Guinevere are scandalously paired as an adulterous couple," she said, as they walked from the Great Room into the Red Room.

Bella looked around, trying to spot Ann in the crowd.

"Look to the right," Lady Malmsby said, pointing. "There are Ann and her duke."

Bella looked in the direction the Duchess pointed, happy to see her friend, Miss Ann Hallowell. "They make an attractive couple," she observed.

"Yes, they do," observed Lady Malmsby, a self-satisfied smile pulling on the corners of her lips that Bella found quite interesting. There was a story here, she was sure of it.

As they approached the couple, she noted they appeared to be discussing the painting hung before them. The oil painting was of the mist at dawn over a pond, just as it is burning away in the rising sunlight.

Lady Oakley leaned toward her. "The Duke painted that."

Bella looked at her, astonished. "Ann's duke? The Duke of Ellinbourne?"

"Yes. He is as talented, some would say more talented, than his uncle."

Bella's brow furrowed. "His uncle?"

"Clarence Wingate."

Bella tilted her head to one side for a moment, then nodded. "That's right, the Wingates of Ellinbourne."

"Yes."

"I saw one of Clarence Wingates' paintings once."

Lady Malmsby laughed. "Yes, of a certainty you did! When you helped us catalog Lady Travis's art collection."

Bella blinked, then blushed at the memory of the painting. *Adam in the Garden of Eden*, the engraved plate on the frame had said.

Lady Malmsby's lips twisted in a sly smile. "And the subject of that painting is Helena's betrothed."

"What?!" Bella shrieked, then looked around. "The subject of the painting is Helena's betrothed?" she whispered, embarrassed to have drawn the attention of those standing nearby.

Lady Malmsby laughed. "Yes. I sense you remember the painting," she observed wryly.

"That is not a painting a person—at least a woman —forgets easily." She vividly remembered the painting. It was a painting of a man standing in full nude glory amongst trees and shrubbery, an apple in his hand. It was also supposed to be a part of one of Candelstone's secret communication transmissions.

"And you say Helena is engaged to the subject of

that painting? He was—I mean—*is* a real person?" she continued.

Lady Malmsby fairly giggled. "Yes. And I might have played a part in both those engagements."

Lady Oakley shook her finger at the Duchess. "Vivian Nowlton, that is a Banbury tale. You were trying to marry off poor Ann to Viscount Redinger."

"Only until I met Ellinbourne," Lady Malmsby defended. "I quickly realized he is perfect for her. I should not have ultimately let her become engaged to Redinger. Totally unsuitable."

Lady Oakley shook her head. "Nonetheless, that was an entertaining house party. I've never been to one quite like it."

"Nor are you ever likely to again," drawled Lady Malmsby.

The ladies laughed together. Bella raised an eyebrow in questioning confusion.

They were almost to the Duke and Ann when Bella saw Aidan Nowlton, Lady Malmsby's son. Her heart clenched in her chest. She should have realized if the Duchess was here, her son would be close by. Of all the people in London, he was the last person she would want to see.

She stopped nearly mid-stride, pulling Lady Malmsby off balance.

"I should find my brother," she abruptly said. "I told him there was enough art in the Great Room to keep me occupied for hours. If I am not in that room and he comes to look for me, he will get anxious," she babbled.

She pulled her arm free from Lady Malmsby and turned to walk back to the main room. Even after three years, the pain of Aidan Nowlton's betrayal ripped through her.

Lady Malmsby grabbed Bella's wrist. "What is the matter? Are you all right?" she asked, concern writ large on her face. "You look like you have seen a ghost."

Bella shook her head. "I have to go. I forgot I told my brother I would meet him in the Great Room," she said again, as if holding on to that notion as a lifeline. "He'll worry if I am not there," she said, pulling free from Lady Malmsby.

She looked back once to where Ann and her Duke stood. They were not alone now. Bella fled the room.

~

AIDAN NOWLTON FROWNED when he saw Lady Isabella Blessingame standing near his mother at the entrance to the Red Exhibit Hall. He warranted she saw him too, and that is why she turned around and precipitously left the room.

As well she should, the deceitful trollop.

He thought they'd had an understanding three years ago. He supposed money, social standing, entertainments, and the excitement of foreign service were more enticing than a mere gallery owner—even if said owner was the brother of a Duke.

But to elope with Sir Harry Blessingame, of all people! His best friend! She'd served him an emotional punch that remained bruised to this day. He rubbed a hand across his sternum as if the flush hit had been delivered yesterday, not three years ago. Not that most people would believe the tall, angular miss had knocked him sideways. He hadn't understood it himself. And he'd never worn his heart on his sleeve. That was not his manner.

He remembered when he first met her, nearly four

years ago. He'd been walking in Hyde Park with his mother. The Duchess liked to walk, said it was excellent exercise that helped keep her young.

Miss Isabella Melville, as she was then, was in the company of Lady Amblethorpe and her youngest daughter, Janine. There had been a winsome shyness in Miss Melville's large dark eyes that vanished the moment Lady Amblethorpe and his mother began speaking of the war effort. She grew quite animated as she told them how she had helped with the war effort. How her brother, knowing how good she was with puzzles and patterns, had brought a captured enemy-coded missive to her to see if she could decipher the message. The best minds at the home office could not do so, and he'd convinced his superior to allow him to give it to her to try. His commanding officer scoffed but allowed him to do so.

It had taken her three days, she'd said, but she'd done it. The message had been about enemy ordnance supply lines. The information she'd deciphered allowed the allies to disrupt the French flow of weapons for their troops. She thought it was fun and hoped she had another opportunity in the future.

They all congratulated her, and she'd radiated her delight. He thought at that moment she was the most beautiful woman he had ever seen.

His mother had wondered if the War Office knew who deciphered the message. They should know, she'd said decisively, so they could understand that women could do more than sew uniforms, wash the laundry, and nurse the injured.

He knew at that moment that his mother would see that Miss Melville received more opportunities to decipher coded messages—even if she used blackmail to make it happen.

And she had.

She had much to answer for.

"Was that Bella with grandmother?" his niece, Ann Hallowell, asked.

"I believe it was," Aidan answered stiffly.

Ann did not hear the reluctance in his voice.

"I haven't seen her since Sicily!" she enthused.

"I wish I hadn't," Aidan said under his breath. The Duke looked at him sharply.

Ann tugged at her fiancé's arm. "Come, let's follow her. I want you to meet her, Miles," she said. "Bella, Helena, and I worked together to catalog Lady Travis's artwork. Will you join us?" Ann asked, turning to Aidan.

He shook his head, though he still stared in Lady Blessingame's direction. "I'm going to finish my review of the room. See if there are any paintings that I might want to offer to sell on commission," he told her. "I'm sure I shall see you later."

Ann Hallowell pulled the Duke of Ellinbourne back toward the Great Room.

"I'm going to try to catch Bella," she said to her grandmother as they came up to her.

"We were bringing Bella to you when she suddenly said she had to go back to the Great Room," Lady Malmsby said. She and Lady Oakley turned back to walk with Ann and Ellinbourne.

"It was the oddest thing," Lady Oakley said. "Her grace pointed to where you were, and she suddenly remembered she'd told her brother she would stay in the main room so he could find her."

Lady Malmsby smirked. "I think it was seeing my son, Aidan, that had her fleeing."

The others looked at her.

Lady Malmsby tilted her head. "Three years ago

they were doing the courting dance, and I was delighted," she told them.

"But when the courtship fell apart, she married Sir Harry Blessingame," Ann said.

Lady Malmsby laughed shortly. "Through the machinations of a spymaster," she said dryly.

"What? Uncle Candelstone?" Ann asked.

Lady Malmsby nodded. "Which resulted from my meddling," the Duchess ruefully admitted with a deep sigh.

"One of your plans gone awry?" Ellinbourne asked Lady Malmsby, amused. The Duchess had a reputation as a meddler and prankster.

"More like a plan that succeeded far beyond my expectations," Lady Malmsby said.

"I thought she came to work for Uncle through her husband," Ann said.

"She did. However, who do you think introduced her to Sir Harry?" Lady Malmsby said.

"Candelstone," said Ellinbourne.

She clasped her hands in front of her. "Precisely. He saw arranging—and preventing—marriages as part of his strategies. Remember when Lord Aldrich married Miss Edgerton, a wool merchant's daughter?"

"Yes," Ellinbourne said slowly, frowning.

"He arranged that marriage after one of Mr. Edgerton's woolen mills burned to the ground in an accident Candelstone inadvertently caused when one of his grand stratagems went awry. It was an expeditious way to appease the merchant and allow Aldrich to look like he was marrying money."

"He wasn't?"

"No, Aldrich was one of Candelstone's agents, who pretended to be an irresponsible gambler. But my point is, this is an example of how Candelstone uses arranged marriages to his convenience. He wanted Bella to work for him, but to do so he needed her married to one of his agents. He didn't pay her, he only paid Sir Harry, and Sir Harry was the only one on the books as employed. She didn't work for Candelstone; however, he considered her an employee, and gave her orders like one."

Ann bit her lower lip, a deep frown pulling her brows together. "I remember when we were in Sicily together, he would call her into the library to give her instructions. I had a sense that she did not want to do what Uncle ordered her to do."

Lady Malmsby nodded. "He grumbled in my hearing of needing to pay her after Harry died. I gave him and my daughter Catherine a dressing-down for that, for they were both of a mind. There was no way Lady Blessingame, as a recent widow, could be in the society company he wished her to be in. She needed her mourning period, and if she was to return to society, she needed more funds than her widow's jointures. And even the lowest peasant gets paid for the work they do, even if it's ha'penny."

"It is no wonder she has been hiding since Waterloo, poor dear," said Lady Oakley.

"But why did she and Mr. Nowlton precipitately leave in opposite directions?" Ellinbourne asked. "You said they were courting, but she chose another. Happens every season. I could understand his animosity if his feelings were more engaged, but she appears to have issues as well. And Nowlton does not strike me as a man to wear the willow. Is she the reason Nowlton has remained a bachelor?"

Lady Malmsby sighed. "I don't know; however, I have my suspicions. Aidan is not an emotional person. Everyone else in the family, in one manner or another, has their heads in the clouds. Aidan is our tether to the ground, like they use for those hot-air balloon exhibitions."

"He does not practice an art?" Ellinbourne asked.

Lady Malmsby and Ann shook their heads. "No, nothing. He loves all art, and that is why he owns a gallery, for he has a most discerning eye; however, he cannot create, only judge and admire," Ann explained.

Ellinbourne frowned. "He is the youngest of your children, correct?"

"Yes," Lady Malmsby said with a smile. "A gift, ten years after Catherine was born."

"By then, everyone had a passion they followed."

"Yes. My daughter Maria, Ann's mother, was a talented watercolorist. Myths and legends enthralled Arthur, Elizabeth found sculpture, and Catherine loved plays and pantomimes, especially the costumes, make-up, and disguises."

Ellinbourne cocked his head to the side. "I would imagine, being the youngest with a significant age gap, the family inadvertently pushed Aidan into a helper role. He didn't have an opportunity to develop his own talents, he was too busy helping everyone with their talents."

Lady Malmsby's brow furrowed. "He takes care of us. He acts more the duke than Arthur does."

"And he is not the heir, Lord Lakehurst is," Ann said.

"My head aches with all these deep thoughts. Let's go to Gunter's for an ice. I could do with sitting down for a while," Lady Malmsby said.

"That sounds delightful! I would love to have one of their sorbets." Lady Oakley said.

"ANDREW, have you finished looking at all the exhibits?" Bella asked when she found her brother in the Great Room.

He nodded. "All the pieces I am interested in," he said. "There is a wonderful collection of paintings and sculptures this year dealing with our illustrious war effort."

"Illustrious for whom," Bella said caustically. "Not illustrious with all the veterans returning home. Especially for those injured without a means to support themselves. And all this art does is romanticize war. There is nothing either romantic or illustrious about war, Andrew," she said bitterly.

He looked at her, his brow furrowing. "What has turned you so sour now? Did you see a particular artwork that disturbed you?"

"More like a particular man."

"Who?"

"Aidan Nowlton," she said.

"I don't understand," he said, a frown pulling at his handsome features.

"I believe Mr. Nowlton would have asked for my hand in marriage if I hadn't married Harry."

Andrew shrugged. "Oh, well, Harry was a splendid chap. And at least you have adequate funds, so you do not need to take a position as a governess or a companion."

Bella rolled her eyes. Her poor brother. "You have no romantic soul, Andrew," she said.

He considered that for a moment. "Yes, that's true. Don't know what I'd do with it if I had one."

"Oh, Andrew. Unfortunately, I know you are not joking."

He shrugged again, unconcerned, then he brightened. "Guess who I met in one of the rooms?"

"I have no idea who that might be that I would know," Bella said dryly.

"Reggie Stafford."

"Candelstone's secretary?"

"Former secretary," her brother said. "Temporarily he's a tutor for Lord Tresham's son. He brought the boy to the Royal Academy today to view the Waterloo paintings."

"That's quite a change in position," Bella said, as they walked around the room. There was art everywhere. Paintings hung so high her neck ached staring up at them.

"Yes, and he's not happy about it. Said he didn't have a chance to ask Lord Candelstone for a reference before he left, and Stafford didn't realize how much Lord Candelstone would be in poor graces with his superiors for how he handled the stolen subsidies affair."

"Allowing the gold and guns intended for our allies to be stolen as a way to capture the traitors was insanity!" Bella said. "But you did all right, if I recall," she added, remembering the stories.

Andrew nodded. "I wasn't in London. I was a military liaison with the smugglers that were helping the war effort—that protected me from the backlash."

"True."

"Did some pretty stupid things following Lord Candelstone's direction as much to the letter as I did. He stressed any means to an end was a fair means to an end. I followed his orders. Thought it would further my career. Almost ruined it."

"But it didn't, and you are an exemplary officer," his sister soothed.

"More like an exemplary messenger boy," he said, disgruntled.

"You are better off out from under Candelstone's eye."

He brightened. "I do like the regiment they have assigned me to."

"At this point in your life, that is what matters," she said.

His head wobbled in indecision. Bella laughed.

"I'd like to return to Mivart's now," she said. "I believe the Duchess of Malmsby will send around a note to invite me to stay with her at Malmsby House until I might find a property to lease."

"Do you wish to do that? She is Nowlton's mother and Candelstone's mother-in-law."

"I know; however, I don't believe I should see them, but nonetheless, I'm willing to risk it to get out of the Mivart Hotel."

"Get out of Mivart's? That is considered the best hotel in London. That's why your solicitor recommended it," Andrew protested.

"Perhaps for a gentleman it is; however, I can attest that they consider any single woman who walks through its doors a light-skirt. Why else would a woman be there?" She said as she steered her brother toward the entrance.

He stopped, forcing Bella to stop. "That is ridiculous! I should speak to the management of the hotel. I am certain that is not an attitude they want to promote."

"They know," she said, urging him forward again. "I have complained. Doesn't do any good. They don't want to alienate any gentlemen who stay there now or would wish to do so over the month. However, I am considering how to drive the point home."

Her brother shrugged. "That's easy. Just tell him your duchess friend was appalled and is having you come to stay with her instead. Won't like that. Guaranteed."

Bella looked at him. "Sometimes, Andrew, you amaze me. That is a brilliant idea."

He shrugged again. "I ain't the smartest fellow, I know that, but it stands to reason. He'd not like to lose potential custom should a duchess put it about how his hotel treated her friend."

Bella tucked her arm in his. "Let's hurry and return to Mivart's. Suddenly my day is looking better."

CHAPTER 2

MALMSBY HOUSE

Bella felt a qualm of misgiving the next morning as she stepped down from the carriage that brought her and her luggage to Malmsby House.

Is it wise to accept the Duchess of Malmsby's invitation to stay here? she asked herself for perhaps the hundredth time. The Duchess was Candelstone's mother-in-law, and Aidan Nowlton's mother. She was bound to meet both gentlemen here. Bella wasn't sure how she felt about those meetings.

Or how she should feel.

Since Harry's death, she'd come to terms with the knowledge Harry had never loved her, nor ever could have loved her. It wasn't in his personality to love anyone beyond himself. He was a great dissembler, which was also what made him a great spy. What she could not understand, and probably never would understand, is why he worked so hard to end the courtship between her and Aidan Nowlton? And afterward, why he wanted to marry her.

The Malmsby House butler swung open the door before Bella could ring the bell.

"Lady Blessingame, to see the Dowager Duchess of Malmsby," she said.

"Yes, my lady," the austere but pleasant butler said, bowing slightly. "Her grace is expecting you. She is waiting just down the hall in the Lady Margaret Parlor. Jimmy here," he said, indicating a footman in dark green livery, "will see to the coachman and have your luggage taken to your room. If you will follow me, I'll take you to her grace."

"Thank you," Bella said, nodding her head slightly in acknowledgment.

She followed the butler down the black-and-white marble tiled floor of the long entrance hall to a pair of doors on the far side, near a bank of windows that looked out to a terrace that ran the length of the house. The terrace abutted a small park-like garden.

"Lady Blessingame, your grace," intoned the butler as he pushed open the white-painted double doors.

The parlor the butler escorted her to was an amazingly ornate pink, white, and gold confection. Not at all what she would have envisioned as favored by Lady Malmsby.

"Bella!" enthused her hostess, her smile bright. Dressed in shades of green, she looked like foliage for the overly pink floral parlor. She held out her hands to Bella, inviting her to sit by her on a strawberry-pink settee. "Mr. Harold," Lady Malmsby said, looking past Bella to the butler. "Please tell Ann that Bella is here. And have refreshments brought in."

The butler bowed. "Right away, your grace," he promised, as he closed the double doors.

"Come in, come in, girl. And do take off that bonnet. Though your blue bonnet is fetching, you are not a visitor expected to leave momentarily. You can put your bonnet, gloves, and reticule on that table, there,"

Lady Malmsby said, pointing to a round table at the other end of the settee.

After Bella placed her things on the table, she turned back toward Lady Malmsby who took her hands in hers.

"I could not help but note that you didn't just leave our company the other day to find your brother, you virtually ran away. Why is that? You must tell me, my dear."

Bella pulled her hands back slightly, but Lady Malmsby held fast. Bella looked away. "La!" she said gaily, turning back toward Lady Malmsby, tossing her head up. "I needed to find my brother. I fear your son-in-law has you seeing intrigues everywhere."

Lady Malmsby raised a skeptical eyebrow. "If I do, then I assure you it is because he is always up to every sort of intrigue imaginable," Lady Malmsby said dryly. "And don't try the gay socialite persona with me. Theatricals were a family enjoyment, with my daughter Catherine leading the amateur productions. Your dissembling won't fadge.— Bella, what is it?" she demanded.

She looked away, damning the sheen of tears that suddenly threatened. "I saw Mr. Nowlton yesterday and realized that, even after three years, I couldn't face him," she said. She turned back to face Lady Malmsby. "So, I ran." She shrugged apologetically. "You see, with the passage of time—and getting to know Harry and his games better," she added with a watery chuckle, "I believe Harry misled me—deliberately misled me so I would reject Mr. Nowlton, which I did with truly hateful words."

Her eyes glistened, threatening her vision. She looked up at the ornate plaster-work ceiling, painted white but finished with the relief glazed in a pale pink wash. She compressed her lips, then a frown creased her brow.

"I felt deeply hurt and confused. But in the last year," she said slowly, consideringly, "I've had time to really think about my life and what has transpired in it. I can truthfully say I am not the young woman you met almost four years ago, or even the one you saw two years ago at Villa Di Fiori. Yesterday, to see Nowlton, memories came rushing back and with it a load of embarrassment and shame."

"I don't understand," said Lady Malmsby. Her eyes narrowed. "No, perhaps I do. Did someone fill your head with stories about my son?"

Bella nodded. "And I was naïve enough to believe him. But he had proof!"

"Him? Who was that? Lord Candelstone?"

"No. It was Harry."

"Sir Harry!" exclaimed Lady Malmsby, "But he was Aidan's best friend throughout their boarding school and university years!"

Bella nodded. "I know. Harry told me."

"What could he possibly say to turn you from Aidan?"

"That Mr. Nowlton was toying with me, that he had some wager in a men's club that he could get under my skirts before the season ended."

"What? That is not Aidan." Lady Malmsby leaned back as she shook her head. "No," she declared. "I don't believe it."

Bella sighed helplessly. "At first, I didn't believe it either, and wondered what game Harry was playing. However, Harry told me of your family's theatrics and how good Aidan was with them. And that was why he was so good as a gallery owner, he said, for he could charm the buyers and the artists. I told him again I didn't believe him, quite forcefully. I believe I even stamped my foot," she said with a slight laugh. "That was not Aidan, I told him. I was quite adamant with him. He told me, his voice full of sympathy, that he understood my resistance. Said Aidan was very good at dissembling."

Lady Malmsby laughed. "Aidan is the worst liar!"

"Well, Harry was a master liar," Bella said. "I saw that in our marriage. He could spin tales for others that I knew were lies, and even *I* could almost believe them!"

"So, how did he convince you that Aidan's behavior was just an act?"

"He said he wrote it in a betting book, and I could have my brother check the book to verify what it said. Andrew looked and told me it was there and that the young bucks were all talking about it."

"My God," said Lady Malmsby. "I still don't believe he would do that." Lady Malmsby's brow furrowed as she shook her head in rejection. "Someone set him up, I'm quite certain," she said forcefully.

"Now, three years later, I agree," Bella said. "But Harry didn't stop with the betting book. He embellished his tale. He reminded me that Aidan was a youngest son and youngest child. The Malmsby properties and monies went to his older brother and to dowries for his three sisters. He said Aidan couldn't marry me. Aidan needed to marry for money. And I knew I had little, not enough for Aidan's needs. I had hoped to find a man who would love me despite my lack of dowry. The knowledge I was being made a fool of because I had no dowry, of being the butt of vile bets, cut me deeply. When these thoughts tumbled over and through me, I remember feeling physically sick. I doubled over and sank to the floor. Harry immediately picked me up and put me upon his lap. He tended to me, said he understood what a bitter pill this was to swallow, but he respected me too much to allow me to continue unawares."

"And it went on from there. Harry insinuated himself into your affections," Lady Malmsby said flatly.

"Yes, but not as much as Aidan had. I told myself that was because Aidan was my first experience with deep emotions, and the first is always the most dramatic."

Lady Malmsby nodded.

"Over time I told myself I loved Harry," Bella said. She smiled. "He was charming. He was fun. He could make any woman he was with feel like they were the center of the universe and he was a peasant at their feet. And he did it all the time. He was not faithful to me. He said it was just part of his work as a spy, that his dalliances with other women meant nothing. I wanted to believe that, but it was hard to watch my husband with these other women and know I was the whispered butt of gossip again. I wanted to believe that Harry really loved me. It was me he married, and it was a game with the other women. And I had myself convinced that was true."

Lady Malmsby shook her head. "I never really trusted Harry—since he was a schoolboy—I could never say why, but it appears my instincts were true. But if I recall, Aidan was upset with you as well."

"Yes, but truly, I didn't listen to the accusations he flung at my head, as angry as I was. I vaguely recall his accusing me of bedding Harry.—Your grace, I am so embarrassed to see Aidan. I know it was over three years; however, when I saw him at the RA, it was like it was yesterday. I still don't know the truth from then, I can only guess, and the biggest question for me is *why!* But that question gnaws at my insides. If Aidan and I were lied to, and we believed those lies, what does that say of either of us, or our feelings for each other, if we could doubt so easily?"

"I don't think you doubted easily if someone went to the trouble of forging Aidan's name to a bet in a betting book! That was carefully planned. But you are correct—the *why* remains the unanswered question, and that is troublesome."

Bella stared back at her hostess and nodded slowly, just as the door to the parlor opened to the maid pushing in a beverage cart, followed by Ann.

"Bella!" Ann joyfully exclaimed. She limped around the maid and threw her arms around Bella just as she was getting up. They fell back on the sofa together, Ann landing on top of Bella.

Lady Malmsby laughed.

Ann scrambled to get off of Bella. "Sorry, sorry!" she said. "But I am so happy to see you!"

"As I am to see you," Bella said as she stood up. "Let's try that again in a proper society scandalizing hug."

"Shall I pour tea, your grace?" the maid asked while the women exchanged hugs.

Ann pulled back from Bella. "Gwinnie will join us," Ann told the maid. "We should wait for her."

"Very good, miss," said the maid. She pushed the cart to the side.

Bella watched Ann as she turned toward her again. Despite the debacle of her courtship with Mr. Nowlton, Ann, Ann's cousin Helena, and she had become friends during their time at Villa de Fiori in Sicily. During the war with Napoleon, Sicily had been under British protection. Lord William Bentinck, the garrison commander of the British troops, had created a small British society with parties, balls, and dinners among the British residents and the Sicilians. It had also been a place plagued with intrigue, owing to its location in the Mediterranean.

It had been a sad time for Bella, with her husband so recently deceased, a death caused by intrigue. However, she'd enjoyed spending time with Ann and her cousin Helena, working together to catalog Lady Travis's art collection. Ann and Helena were the first female friends Bella had had since she married Harry. Spy work did not lend itself to close friendships, she caustically acknowledged to herself.

"I am so glad you have come to stay with Grandmother," Ann said. "I'm staying here as well with my stepmother, Ursula, until after the ball."

"Will Mrs. Hallowell also be joining us for tea?" Lady Malmsby asked.

"I don't think so. She had another crying spell this morning and claims to be tired and in need of a nap."

Ann turned to Bella. "My stepmother had a gentleman friend she was most enchanted with, then she discovered he met her because Uncle Candelstone wished him to meet her and squire her about."

"Why?"

Lady Malmsby laughed, "Because Ann is my granddaughter and he hoped, through Ursula and Colonel Brantley's relationship, he would get an invitation to my country house. Which he did. Ursula learned this and has been depressed since then, though Colonel Brantley swears he now loves her."

The door to the parlor opened again. A giantess with gloriously rich, dark red hair and a solid, voluptuous figure entered.

"I'm sorry for keeping you waiting!" she said. "You should have gone on without me."

"Nonsense," said Lady Malmsby. She looked toward Bella. "Bella, this is another of my granddaughters, Lady Guinevere Nowlton. Gwinnie, this is Lady Isabella Blessingame. She will stay with us for a few days as her estate agent scours London for a suitable lodging to rent."

"Welcome," Lady Guinevere responded in a surprisingly deep, resonating voice.

Bella liked her instantly.

"In our family of talents, Gwinnie is our musician," Lady Malmsby said, as she pulled the covering from the tea service. "Milk and sugar?" she asked Bella.

"Just milk, please," Bella said. She watched, bemused, as Lady Guinevere pulled up one of the room's upholstered chairs to join their group without calling for a servant to do the task.

"What instrument do you play?" Bella asked Lady Guinevere.

"Most any stringed instrument," Lady Guinevere said breezily, as she flopped into the chair she'd dragged forward. "Though my instrument of choice is the violin. I also play the pianoforte. Do you play?" she asked her.

Bella laughed. "Sadly, no. That was a portion of a lady's education that I missed."

"Well, I shan't hold it against you. I ask most everyone I meet, as I am always searching for volunteers for concerts," Lady Guinevere said as she accepted a cup of tea from her grandmother.

"I think you mean conscripts," said Lady Malmsby dryly.

Lady Guinevere smiled, but otherwise compressed her lips as she mischievously looked up and away, her eyes laughing. She looked back. "What can I say? I love music and I get enjoyment from playing. And—" looking with a mock glare at her grandmother, "I'm quite disgruntled that they will not let me play at Ann's betrothal ball," she confessed to Bella.

"You can't be the hired help at your cousin's ball!" Lady Malmsby mildly protested.

Lady Guinevere gave an unladylike *harrumph*. "Yes, then I should like you by my side when I am introduced about, to give me the aside information—"

"Gossip," Lady Malmsby clarified for Bella with an arched look.

Ann frowned at her grandmother. "Well, I don't know most of the society invited, either."

"It was your decision not to attend social events, Ann. Ursula has always been a regular attendee, and I know if they invited her, you were invited as well."

Ann screwed up her nose. "I'd just rather paint or read a book."

"And that is why you are well-matched with Ellinbourne."

Ann smiled. "True," she said, with the wistfulness of a woman in love.

"Well, I, for one, would still like to attend one of your concerts, Lady Guinevere." Bella said, raising her teacup for a sip of tea.

Lady Guinevere fluttered her hand about dismissively. "Oh, please, call me Gwinnie, as the family does. We aren't very good with titles," she confessed, scrunching her nose. "Father is more of an academic than a duke. You shall see. He doesn't have a formal bone in his body, much to the dismay of his strawberry-leaf compatriots. It will be a chore to get him dressed properly for the ball and primed to address the guests appropriately," she told Bella.

Lady Malmsby sighed. "He is my son, and I must

admit there is truth in my granddaughter's words. Though sometimes I detect a certain glint in his eyes and wonder what goes on behind those spectacles he wears. All of my children were so unique and different from one another. That has been a delight for me, but has confused society."

"But as far as receiving an invitation, as you are in town now, and staying here, Lady Amblethorpe will welcome you to her musicale. It is the day before the ball. I shall be playing there with a mixed assortment of musicians," she said with a laugh.

"Do you remember, Bella? I first met you while you were out walking with Lady Amblethorpe and her daughter, Janine."

"Yes, I remember," Bella said. "Her mother sadly ruled Janine, as I recall."

"No longer. Janine is now the Countess of Havelock. For the last eight or nine months now," Lady Malmsby said.

Bella's eyes widened. "I shall have to write her! And I shall certainly look forward to Lady Amblethorpe's party," she said.

"Lady Amblethorpe is unique among society matrons. She does not give balls, she does musicales," Gwinnie went on. "Does well with them, too. People willingly attend. I can't say the same for all society musicale functions. She has only had one misstep that I can recall in her musical programs."

"Oh yes, that hideous singer that her son talked her into sponsoring," Lady Malmsby said. "The one with the fake Italian accent."

Gwinnie shrugged. "I don't know about the accent. I know she couldn't hit a proper note. I shudder at that memory; however, I enjoy playing at Lady Amblethorpe's musicales. The guests are attentive to the music. That is rare."

"What will you be playing?" Bella asked.

She shrugged. "The works of Pagani, I think. Maybe a Vivaldi. We shall see how the time goes," she said, before popping the last small confection from her plate into her mouth.

"These confections are quite good, Grandmother, but I should grow to be as big as a house if we continue to have these every day with tea, and I am already large enough as it is, without adding breadth to my height!"

Lady Malmsby smiled, perking up. "They are quite good, aren't they? But you know, you don't have to eat them."

"Not eat them? That would be sacrilegious to not eat these, as good as they are. Better that he not make them," Gwinnie said.

"She."

"I beg your pardon?"

"She. My chef is a woman."

Gwinnie clapped her hands. "That is wonderful! Do you think she would consider leaving your employ to take over the kitchen here?"

"Trying to poach my staff?"

"We often have the most uninspired meals," Gwinnie lamented. "Meat and potatoes, overcooked. Hardly appropriate fare for a ducal household, but Father doesn't mind. I don't think he even notices what he eats, as his nose is often in a book he has brought to the table."

"No! I taught him better than that!"

Bella loved the interplay amongst the Nowlton relations. That wasn't part of her background. She felt a twinge of envy for what she missed in her life.

Gwinnie shrugged, then set her napkin on the tea tray and rose to her feet. "I received some music in the mails today that I am eager to play. I hope you will excuse me. I shall see you at supper."

"I should like to go to my room as well," Bella said.

"Oh, gracious yes, you haven't even been there yet, have you?" said Lady Malmsby. Gwinnie, could you show Bella to her room? We've put her in the green bedroom."

"Certainly!" said the exuberant Gwinnie. "I'd be delighted to."

"Thank you!" Bella said, rising from her seat. She grabbed her bonnet and things and hurriedly followed Gwinnie, who fairly bounced as she walked.

"It is a bit of a distance," Gwinnie told her as she shut the parlor door behind them. "It seems everything in this house is a bit of a distance away from wherever you want to be," she said ruefully.

"That's not a worry. Having lived in the country for the past year, I am accustomed to walking," Bella told her.

"I envy you that. Father is very much a city person. Other than the occasional trip to grandmother's Versely Park estate, I've only been in London."

"Oh, no! You shall have to visit me at my Lennox Hill estate. I'd wager you would love going out in the hills to play your violin in nature."

"I've never considered playing outside," Gwinnie said, thoughtfully.

"How could you, being in the city with the smoke and noise?" Bella said. "The countryside is vastly different."

"That sounds like a fascinating proposition."

They were walking up the broad, carpeted staircase when the front door opened, and Aidan Nowlton entered.

Bella froze when she saw him. Memories flooded her. She stared at him, feeling strangely lost.

He was more of an arresting figure now than he had been three years ago. Not a handsome man; however, sometimes handsome looked banal without the character to complement the pretty face. Not Aidan Nowlton. Strong-featured, he was a man to be noted. The hint of gray she now saw along his temples gave him an air of sophistication and sharpened his appeal.

The sudden ache in her chest surprised her, for she also remembered the stinging of the words he said to her at their last meeting, accusing her of lifting her skirts to any gentleman who came her way. Even Harry. That she had been a trollop, leading him on. His words had cut her like whip lashes. She should hate him, but hate did not exist in the maelstrom of emotions that churned within her.

She looked away from him and hurried after Gwinnie.

～

AIDAN NOWLTON STRIPPED off his gloves, then took off his high-crowned beaver hat and handed both to a waiting footman.

He scowled as he watched Lady Isabella Blessingame ascend the stairs in his niece's wake. What was she doing here?

Three years ago, Aidan had requested permission to court Isabella Melville. That had been the worst mistake of his life.

"Do you know where my mother is?" he asked the footman, his tone harsh.

When he saw the footman's surprised expression at his tone, he relaxed his face. He should not let anger from years past influence his behavior today. The past was the past. "I have some news about a piece of art she might like to add to her collection," he said in a neutral tone, shoving the emotions that unexpectedly swamped him back into his mind's attic, where they belonged, gathering dust.

"She's in the Lady Margaret Parlor, sir."

Aidan nodded and walked down the long entrance hall. He'd felt a familiar ache in his gut when he saw Bella. He couldn't fathom why he still reacted to her after three years. She had lied to him and betrayed him with his best friend. He should have moved on with his life, yet she haunted him. There had not been another woman since her, and he feared there might never be if he couldn't purge her from his soul.

He knocked lightly on the parlor door, then let himself in. His mother was with Ann, finishing tea. No doubt discussing wedding plans. Maybe it was Ann's wedding that was plaguing him so. Three years ago, he had hoped to be planning his own wedding. Why wouldn't the emotions remain in their attic storage? Seeing Bella only made them sharper.

"Mother, what is Lady Blessingame doing here?" he asked, then cursed himself for blurting out that question as soon as he entered the room. That was not a way to purge the woman from his mind.

"She's staying here for a while," his mother said calmly. She sipped her tea.

"No!" he fairly roared before he could consider his reaction. His left hand tightened into a fist. Why couldn't he stop?

Lady Malmsby frowned. She set her cup down. "Aidan, what has gotten into you?"

Even his niece, Ann, looked at him as some unknown creature.

He took a deep breath, then sat in the chair Lady
Guinevere had brought forward at a right angle to
where his mother sat on the bright pink settee. He
slowly uncurled his fingers and stretched them out on
his knee to loosen his tension. He repeated the action,
but it didn't help.

"You know what happened three years ago," he
said tightly.

"Yes, you wished to marry Bella; however, she
chose another to wed," Lady Malmsby said.

Ann looked, wide-eyed, from one to the other.

"You make it sound so simple. It was anything but
simple," Aidan said tiredly, struggling to get himself in
hand.

"Only because you choose to make it so. Both of
you choose to make it so. It is a bumble broth, to be
sure. You should sit down and talk to her."

"Not in bloody hell," he snapped. He placed his
head in his hands as he lowered his head, his elbows
resting on his knees. "My apologies, Mother, Ann."

"Seriously, you should talk to her. What you think
happened is not what happened. And it did not just
happen to you, it happened to Bella as well."

"No, I do not wish to talk about history, not with
you or her. That was three years ago. My life has
moved on."

"But Aidan—" began his mother.

"No!" he said explosively, sitting up straight. "No,"
he repeated in a calmer voice. "Please, no."

Lady Malmsby leaned back and looked at him.
"All right, I won't. Not today at least."

"Never," Aidan ground out.

Lady Malmsby frowned, ready to argue, but took a

breath instead when Ann laid a hand on her arm. She looked at her granddaughter, then turned back to Aidan. "All right," she said, her lips pursed. "So, what brings you here today? We did not expect to see you until the ball."

"Art, of course," he said, his voice now modulated. He glanced over at his niece and nodded slightly, grateful for her intrusion. He didn't want to argue with his mother. He also did not want to talk about Isabella Blessingame.

"Peter Hampton has approached me to sell his painting that is currently on display in the Royal Academy Exhibition."

"And you're wondering if I'd like to add one of his pieces to my collection," she said.

"You had mentioned at one time you liked his style."

"I do. He does romanticism with an edge. I like it, but what I haven't liked since his debut is his lifestyle. I think he will burn out too fast. However, if it will help get it sold, you can bruit it about that I am considering it. I always consider. That may cause someone to jump on it ahead of me."

"Grandmother, you are devious," said Ann.

"It is part of my charm," Lady Malmsby replied.

Aidan doubled over with laughter. "Truer words have never been said," he finally got out as he wiped his eyes. He rose to his feet. "Thank you for that touch of comedic relief. I needed that today. Thank you. With that, I take my leave of you. I shall see you the night of the ball."

"You are not attending Lady Amblethorpe's musicale"

"Not this time."

"Aidan, based on the feelings you displayed earlier,

I feel I must warn you that Lady Blessingame will be at the ball. You cannot avoid her the entire time she is in London. I trust you will have time before then to marshal your thoughts and not embarrass yourself— or her—with antipathy."

He compressed his lips tightly, but knew she spoke wisely. He nodded curtly. "I can assure you I shall have myself in hand. The question is, will she?"

Jimmy, the footman Bella recognized from earlier, directed her to the parlor where the family gathered before meals. It was a lovely, high-ceilinged room done in soft blue and white with tastefully refined touches of gold. A perfect decor to relax in prior to a meal.

There was already someone in the room when she walked in. A giant to Gwinnie's giantess. This must be her brother, Lord Lakehurst. He was even taller than his twin, Gwinnie. A smooth-shaven, dauntingly large man with broad shoulders and wavy dark red hair that blazed with fiery highlights in the chandelier candlelight. She could imagine him as a medieval warrior, wearing a kilt and brandishing a claymore.

But he was formally dressed in black evening attire, which made Bella feel underdressed for dinner, not that she had many choices in the wardrobe she'd judged to bring with her to London. She hadn't expected to be socializing, let alone staying at the home of a duke.

He smiled when he saw her, his smile lighting his entire face, just as Gwinnie's did hers. Definitely siblings.

"You must be Lady Blessingame," he said in a

smooth, deep voice. "The Duke asked me to pass on his apologies to you. He will not be here at dinner this evening to meet you. He is in Richmond attending some lecture. I don't know which one. They all sound so dreadfully boring I've stopped asking."

Bella laughed, as she knew he meant her to.

Lord Lakehurst led her to a blue jacquard sofa. "May I get you a preprandial?" he asked.

"Yes, that would be lovely."

"Ratafia or sherry?"

"I prefer sherry," she said.

"I will remember that," he said as he picked up a cut crystal decanter and removed the glass stopper.

"Lake, would you pour me a glass as well?" asked Lady Malmsby, as she and Gwinnie entered the room.

"And I would prefer my ratafia."

"I know, Sister, my dear. Would you come help serve?"

Gwinnie went to join Lord Lakehurst at the beverage cart to pick up the glasses for Lady Malmsby and herself. Bella marveled at how alike they looked for brother and sister. She was relieved to see Gwinnie was not dressed in as formal an attire as her brother. She wore a teal gown with slight ruching on the bodice and cream lace edging. Her attire displayed restrained elegance that clearly suited her height.

Lady Malmsby sat down next to Bella.

"I just told Lady Blessingame that the Duke will not be joining us this evening."

"Another lecture?" Lady Malmsby asked resignedly.

Lord Lakehurst inclined his head, "Of course." He handed Bella her glass while Gwinnie handed one to Lady Malmsby.

"Then there will only be the four of us for dinner,

as Ann and Mrs. Hallowell are joining Ellinbourne and his family tonight for dinner," Lady Malmsby said.

"That is wonderful," Lord Lakehurst said as he took a chair. "Then we shall have our lovely guest all to ourselves and I get to ask all manner of questions."

Lady Malmsby turned to Bella. "I should have warned you about Lake."

"Warn anyone about me? You make me sound like some dastardly fellow," Lord Lakehurst protested.

Gwinnie and Lady Malmsby laughed.

"My brother is an author. A novelist," Gwinnie said. "He is currently in the midst of writing his third or fourth novel, I forget."

"You wound me, Gwinnie, that you don't know that this is my fourth," Lord Lakehurst said.

"What do you write? Are any published?" Bella asked.

"They published two, and the third is due out later this month, according to the publisher," he said. "I write Gothic fiction."

"Under the name *Anonymous*," Gwinnie put in.

"Why Anonymous?" Bella asked.

"Because my publisher was of the mind it would provide more salacious mystery and therefore more sales."

"Has it?"

Lord Lakehurst shrugged. "I have nothing to compare it to, so I don't know. However, I will say sales have been generous, so I am not inclined to mess with a winning formula."

"So are your books salacious?" she asked.

"Not particularly so," he said thoughtfully, "at least not in the milieu of Gothic."

"He likes demons and cults," Gwinnie confided.

"That is true," Lord Lakehurst said. "At least at the moment."

"Excuse me, your grace, my lord and ladies," said Mr. Harold from the doorway. "Dinner is served."

"Excellent, I am famished," Lord Lakehurst said as he rose from his chair. "Grandmother?" he said as he offered his arm to her. "Lady Blessingame, would you care to take my other?" he asked.

"I will," Bella said affably.

"How come you never offer me your arm?" Gwinnie mockingly complained.

"Because you are you," her brother said, leading the Dowager Duchess and Bella into the dining room.

With only four for dinner, the seating was casual, and conversation easily flowed among them.

"What brought you to London at this time of year, so late in the Season?" Lord Lakehurst asked Bella.

"Primarily, my solicitor—or rather, my late husband's solicitor. He summoned me to London." She made a face. "He said there was a codicil in Harry's will that said it wasn't to be read until he had been deceased two years."

"It's been over two years, as we've been back from Sicily for over two years," Lady Malmsby said.

"Yes, doesn't say much for them as solicitors, does it," Bella drawled. "And the wording in the letter was quite peremptory. That did not agree with me well, either. But I thought it best to heed their summons and come. I was supposed to meet with him two days ago; however, he sent round a note saying to defer until tomorrow. To say I will acquire the services of a different solicitor when this is over is an understatement. The second reason I am in London is to personally tell Lord Candelstone to leave me alone," Bella told them.

"What is Silly Willy doing now?" Lord Lakehurst asked.

"Silly Willy?" Bella repeated.

"That is my fault," said Lady Malmsby. "He was a neighbor growing up and always around. He made the silliest pronouncements, swearing they were the truth. I started calling him Silly Willy. This was years ago. Naturally, I stopped when I discovered Catherine's tendre for the man, but sometimes he makes my head hurt in exasperation. One day, when I was particularly exasperated with him, I repeated that name in Lake's hearing and to my lasting dismay, that is now the name he insists on using. Proves the adage you can't say anything around children—even twenty-seven-year-old children."

Lord Lakehurst grinned at her. "But it is so *à propos!*"

"Please desist, Lake. Remember, he is your aunt's husband. You should show some respect."

"Maybe... someday," Lord Lakehurst said, shrugging. "But tell us, Lady Blessingame, your experiences with my uncle."

"Sir Harry Blessingame, my husband, was one of Lord Candelstone's agents abroad."

"A spy."

"Yes, a spy. And as Harry's wife, I assisted his work by providing cryptography for captured coded French communiques. When Harry died, Lord Candelstone convinced me to carry on his work, including the code-breaking and spying on the Spanish envoy in Brussels, Vizconde Miguel Carrasco-Torres. I did, but after Waterloo I quit. He wants me to come back and work for him again."

"But I thought he had retired—or as rumors said, been forced to retire." Lord Lakehurst said.

"He had," said Lady Malmsby. "It appears he is trying to form a private network of spies. That is what we discovered last month at my house party. I really should request he be given an overseas assignment far, far away. I just can't bring myself to do that to Catherine."

"Sic Aidan on the problem," Lord Lakehurst offered casually.

Bella cocked her head. "Why would you say to sic Mr. Nowlton on him? I know they don't like each other, but what would you have Nowlton do?"

"Oh, I don't know, but he'd figure out something. He always does when we need something done."

Gwinnie nodded. "Uncle Aidan is our fix-it person. We need a problem solved, we need something done that is distasteful or boring to do, we ask Aidan to do it."

"Why?" Bella asked.

Gwinnie shrugged. "It's what he's always done, isn't that right, Grandmother?"

"Yes. As a child, Aidan didn't display any particular talent, like his siblings, and he wanted to be good at something like they were. So, he asked what he could do to help us with our talents. And he did. He seemed to enjoy helping, so we have let him continue that habit. But I admit, Ellinbourne said something the other day that has had me wondering if we didn't cause Aidan not to develop his own talent."

"What do you mean?" asked Lord Lakehurst.

"Ellinbourne suggested Aidan didn't have a chance to develop his own talent—whatever that might be—as he was too busy helping everyone with their talents."

"He is a wonder at getting things done," Gwinnie said.

"I did not know," Bella said. "He is very discreet, isn't he?"

"Yes. One may trust Aidan to keep one's secrets for you. All part of his service to the family."

Bella frowned.

"What is it, my dear?" asked Lady Malmsby.

Bella shook her head. "I'm just thinking of some things." She was thinking she felt a great deal of sympathy for Aidan.

As soon as dinner was over, Lord Lakehurst excused himself. He was going to the theater with some of his cronies, and, from Bella's inference, she gathered he had arranged an assignation for afterward—thus the formal attire.

She, Lady Malmsby, and Gwinnie shared an after-dinner drink, then bid each other goodnight, far earlier than usual society hours. Gwinnie said she was going to practice for a couple of hours, and Lady Malmsby said she had correspondence to complete. This left Bella at loose ends. She didn't mind. She had a great deal to think about.

When Bella met Aidan Nowlton three years ago, one of the aspects of his personality that drew her to him was his courteousness and how he was always doing things for his family. Three years ago, she'd found that endearing. Now she thought his family used Nowlton unfairly. And to say he lacked talents? Bella disagreed. His talents weren't tangible, like painting, sculpting, and writing. Nowlton had an uncanny sense for art. He knew what it was when he saw it, and what it wasn't. A well-defined Art Aesthetic, particularly for the romanticism movement. And if, as a younger son, Nowlton had pursued a commission, he would have been an able commander and strategist. Most likely directly on Wellington's staff.

His life had gone a different path from those around him, but he had used his strengths. That was interesting.

She had seen a bit of this in him during their courtship. She remembered, with a sad secret smile, three years ago when he requested permission to court her. Her heart had fluttered wildly. A thousand butterflies could not have raised more of a fluttering sensation. Painfully shy, she appreciated his courtesy. He was gentle, but keenly interested in all she said. He made her feel like the smartest woman in London. She enjoyed her time spent with him and wondered when he might offer for her.

She sighed.

Thanks to Harry, he hadn't, and they'd lost that promise of tomorrow.

CHAPTER 3

HARGATE, OWEN, AND HARGATE

B ella stood hesitantly at the door of the breakfast parlor the next morning. One person sat in the room. He had the look of Aidan Nowlton, but older and on a larger frame. Spectacles sat on his nose as he read a book open beside his plate.

When he noticed her standing there, he closed the book and rose to his feet.

"Good morning! You must be Lady Blessingame. Allow me to introduce myself. I am Arthur Nowlton, Duke of Malmsby," he said, bowing slightly. "Come in, come in, please. Jimmy here will get you a plate," he said, indicating the footman who stood next to the breakfast buffet.

Bella sat in a chair near the Duke as he resumed his own.

"I'm sorry I missed meeting you at dinner last night. I was pledged to a lecture in Richmond last evening and had left early to have dinner there before the lecture.—In truth, I didn't feel like taking a carriage ride on a full stomach," he confided, with a merry wink.

"I can't say I blame you," she said. "So, what are

you reading? I notice it is a new book. Has there been more written about King Arthur?"

"No, no—at least, I don't think so." He whispered. "Actually, don't tell my family, however, I have done nothing with King Arthur in several years. Not since my wife died. She was the King Arthur enthusiast."

Bella sat up straighter. "Oh! They led me to believe that is all you do is study and write about King Arthur."

He shook his head. "Rubbish. Don't get me wrong, I'm actually quite fond of the old guy; however, I exhausted my sources and interest. On to other things now. There is so much to learn in this world, and so little time. This book," he said, holding up the book, "is *A History of Persia* by Sir John Malcolm. Just light breakfast reading."

"Is all the reading and studying you do the reason you leave your social obligations to your son? I heard Lord Lakehurst talking about them last night."

He shook his head. "No, no." He took up his napkin to wipe his mouth. "Only way to get him out in society to meet a gel he might like to marry. If he didn't get out and about, he'd live in his fantastical writing worlds.—And I can see you are a bright woman, so before you ask, I'll tell you. No one knows I don't work on Arthurian stuff any longer because they don't ask," he said, rising from the table.

"Oh!"

"I'm off now to have a demonstration and study of a new steam engine. Love those things and what they are building with them. And Jimmy," he said, turning to the footman, "You know what to tell the family if they ask?"

"You are at the library, your grace," the footman dutifully responded.

He turned back to Bella and winked again, then he was gone, leaving Bella bemused. Does everyone live with secrets?

Bella had just requested a coffee refill when Lady Malmsby and Gwinnie came into breakfast.

"Good morning, Bella!" Lady Malmsby said. "I'm glad I caught you here. We have decided, Gwinnie and myself, that Gwinnie will accompany you to the solicitor's office today."

"Thank you, your grace, but that won't be necessary, and I know Gwinnie would rather be practicing."

"I'm serious, Bella. You need another pair of eyes and ears to hear all the solicitor will say. It is not common for a solicitor to *summon* a client to visit, particularly if said client is out of town, then leave them kicking their heels for two days. That shows a lack of respect that is not acceptable."

"And I said to Grandmother that if there is unfinished business from two years ago, they are incompetent, thieves, or Sir Harry played some tricks with his will and your inheritance. A disinterested third party can help sort the details and suggest questions you might not consider as you think about what you learn."

Bella thought about what they said. "I do not believe it is the first two," she said slowly. "But I could well believe the third. I admit, a person who doesn't know Harry might be an advantage at this meeting."

Gwinnie bounced on her toes. "I'm looking forward to the outing! I confess, I have a curiosity about all legal things. When I'm not playing music, I like to sit in the gallery at the Olde Bailey and listen to the legal proceedings. They are all so fascinating. More enjoyable than rounds of visiting. The trials bore my maid, Rose, but she brings knitting with her. I get so complacent, one day much like the other. I suggested to Grandmother that I go with you. Grandmother had quite decided that *she* would accompany you. I told her I did not think that was a good idea. She would take over your meeting and you wouldn't like that."

"Unfortunately, I agree with Gwinnie. I have that tendency," Lady Malmsby ruefully said. "Typically, this is something I would ask Nowlton to do, as he is whom I first turn to whenever I have a legal question or issue. However, understanding your mutual feelings toward each other, I can't do that."

"I would not have gone with him!" Bella said. "And I would go back to Mivart's Hotel before I would allow you to throw me into his company."

Lady Malmsby nodded. "I know, I won't do that, and it appears Nowlton is of the same mind as you." She compressed her lips momentarily. "I never confronted Nowlton three years ago as to what went on. I should have. That was remiss on my part."

"And quite unlike you," Gwinnie adds.

Lady Malmsby frowned at her but nodded in reluctant agreement.

SHORTLY BEFORE 10:00 A.M., Stephen, the footman, assisted Bella, Gwinnie, and Gwinnie's maid, Rose, into a Malmsby carriage for the journey across town to the offices of Hargate, Owen, and Hargate.

"I know little about the law practiced by solicitors," Gwinnie told Bella. "From what I've read, it can be boring. It is the barristers who come before judges who fascinate me. They, and the magistrates and Bow Street Runners who bring miscreants to trial. The stories one hears in a courtroom are horrifying."

"If they are horrifying, why do you go?"

She lifted her shoulders slightly, then dropped them. "I don't know," she said. She looked out the carriage window. "I've lived a sheltered life. I believe most of the aristocracy do. And in my case, I have a father who lives in the past and a brother who, through his gothic novels, lives in make-believe. A horrifying make-believe sometimes, but nonetheless make-believe. I look out in the streets and see people engaged in all manner of activities and I wonder about them. Then I went to my first trial. Remember it Rose?" Gwinnie asked, looking over at her maid.

"Indeed, I do, my lady, shameful, it were," Rose said, looking up from her knitting.

Gwinnie nodded. She turned back to Bella. "The footman, Stephen, who helped us into the carriage, had a nephew kidnapped for his clothes."

"A child kidnapped for their clothes?"

"Yes. Sometimes even infants are kidnapped, stripped of their clothes and left somewhere with just a nappy on while the kidnapper sells the tyke's clothes in the pawnshops. Most times just for the price of a bottle of blue ruin.

"Most times the kidnapper thieves are not caught —this once they were. A laundress. Rose and I went to the trial."

Rose nodded. "And she showed no remorse, neither. Ungodly woman."

Gwinnie nodded. "And it wasn't the first time she'd done this for drink. The proceedings and the other cases heard the same day fascinated me. I've passed many afternoons in the galleries since then. What people do, and why they do it is sometimes heartbreaking. Sometimes it is just to survive. I work with a small group of like-minded peers. We support homes and education for those who have found themselves so desperate or threatened that they have resorted to crime, but in their souls are good people."

"You gladden my heart to hear there are such people in our society. My experiences have not shown the same kindness to others," Bella said, bitterly remembering all she'd seen in the war.

Gwinnie sighed, "Unfortunately, not enough.—We are getting close to the area of town where your solicitor has an office."

"I am glad one of us knows their way around the city," Bella said, smiling. Then she sobered. "I should be glad to have behind me whatever he has to tell me. I want that part of my life done and over with," Bella strongly said.

Gwinnie's maid looked across at her with an expression Bella couldn't fathom, but suddenly she felt wary of the woman.

The ducal arms on the carriage doors drew a small crowd of curious passersby. Bella mused that their presence in front of Hargate, Owen, and Hargate may raise the local status of the solicitors. She allowed the groom who'd ridden at the back of the carriage to help her down.

When they walked through the door into the office, she was pleased with what she saw—a neat, respectable law firm office. With Harry, it was sometimes hard to know whom he would take his business to.

Three clerks sat at a long pine table, books scattered on the table next to and on top of stacks of papers. Only one—the youngest, by appearance—looked up and rose as they entered.

"How might we help you?" the young man said, bowing slightly.

"I have an appointment with Mr. Hargate," Bella said. "I am Lady Isabella Blessingame, and this is Lady Guinevere Nowlton."

The young man looked from one to the other and at Gwinnie's maid standing behind them. "He was only expecting you, Lady Blessingame," the young man said uncertainly.

"Did you truly expect a woman to come here alone," Gwinnie demanded, looking down her nose at the man in much the manner of her grandmother.

"Yes, no! Of course not, but—"

"There is no *but*," Bella interrupted. "Inform Mr. Hargate we are here, and arrange a chair for Lady Guinevere's maid to await us out here."

"Immediately, my lady," the young man said, his voice breaking slightly. "If you'll follow me," he said, leading them to a door in the back corner. "Michael," he bawled out over his shoulder, "give the maid your chair!" Then he looked at them sweetly and opened the door. It led to a hallway to the back of the building and to a stairway landing. He led them up the narrow, steep stairs that opened onto a large, sunlit room. Bookshelves covered every spare space of the wall that did not have a window. Papers and worn, leather-bound books were stacked everywhere, including the hearth space that was now cold due to summer. A pine solicitor's hutch sat behind the desk, while at the desk sat a tall man with a fringe of gray hair like a tonsured monk. He might have faded back into the bookshelves that lined the long, narrow office if it weren't for his crimson jacquard waistcoat. He sat almost hidden behind the stacks of papers, some bound together, others in slip-shod towers ready to fall over across his wide desk.

"Lady Blessingame and Lady Guinevere Nowlton

to see you, sir," the young law clerk said from the top of the stairs.

The man jerked his head up. "Two ladies?" he asked.

"Yes," Bella said from the top of the stairs, "surely you did not expect me to come to your place of business without companionship. To complete the niceties, Lady Guinevere's maid is with us, at the moment, settled in your front office." She swept past their escort upstairs and made her way into the office. Gwinnie followed close behind.

Bella stood before the man's desk for a moment, but when he said nothing, just looked at her, bemused, she made a show of spreading her skirts out as she sat in the chair across from him. Gwinnie sat next to her. "Now, sir, you will explain to me why you summoned me to London and the situation we have before us. I was not pleased to receive your summons. I found it arrogant in the extreme for several reasons."

She raised a gloved hand to tick off reasons on her fingers.

"One. Sir Harry has been dead for some time. Two. Only now, years later, you request I come to London to meet you to discuss additional aspects regarding Harry's will, implying you hadn't been totally forthcoming at the time of his death. Aside from this, I find it the height of rudeness for you to demand I come to you. If I hadn't already been planning to return to London, I would have ignored your—how should I put it—summons? Three. You *dictate* the day and hour for the meeting, then when I arrive, you put me off for two days. Four. You arranged for me to stay in a hotel that you assured me was the height of propriety, yet proved otherwise. While there I was the subject of various rude and crude importuning. And five. Judging by your clerk's attitude, you assumed I would come alone, though why, I cannot conceive."

Bella tossed her head up. "I am forced to wonder, just what sort of woman do you believe me to be?"

From the doorway came clapping. Bella and Gwinnie turned to see a well-set-up man in an exquisitely tailored gray suit.

"I told you, Father, you are ham-handed," the man laconically said, looking at Mr. Hargate seated at the desk, hunched lower behind his stacks of paper.

"Excuse me, ladies," the man said, bowing slightly. "I am Richard Hargate, the second Hargate of Hargate, Owen, and Hargate. The clerk downstairs said you are Lady Blessingame and Lady Guinevere Nowlton?" he said, his voice rising to a question.

Bella inclined her head.

"Excellent," he said. He languidly stripped off his gloves, then tucked his gloves in his hat, and set the hat atop a bookshelf by the door. He looked about the office, then selected a stack of papers on the desk to move to the floor and sat on the corner of the desk he'd cleared.

"Now, I feel I must tell you that my father is an excellent solicitor, but doesn't do well with people, especially of the feminine variety. Sometimes I find it astounding that he ever married and had issue at all."

The older man jerked his head up at that statement and glared at his son over his wire-framed glasses.

"My mother was a saint," the younger Mr. Hargate continued. Behind him, his father frowned, but nodded.

Bella didn't know why it would be so; however, that single reaction from the senior Mr. Hargate made her feel much more in charity with him.

Richard Hargate cocked his head to the side as he leaned forward, staring at Lady Guinevere. "Excuse me, my lady, you look familiar to me, but I can't place from where. I am typically quite good at remembering people."

Bella saw Gwinnie blush.

"Mrs. Southerlands," Gwinnie softly responded.

"Ah, yes. My apologies, Lady Guinevere. I should have realized the woman helping Mrs. Southerlands was incognito, and I have gone and spoiled that," Mr. Hargate said. He crossed his hands atop each other on his knee as he straightened.

"It's all right if Bella knows." She turned to Bella. "I help young women—primarily young girls from the country who have had a misfortune—to better themselves. I help them read and do their numbers so they might get positions in genteel retail establishments, or as maids. A duke's daughter would render some tongue-tied. I needed to have them be comfortable working with me. They know me as Sarah Knolls."

"That's wonderful!" Bella enthused. "How did you come to that?"

Gwinnie smiled. "Through the *dour* Earl of Soothcoor," she said. "That is what people call him, as he seldom smiles. He is quite involved with the charities in the city."

"And farther afield," Mr. Hargate said. "I assist him with some of the legal paperwork for his charitable interests," he explained.

"But I beg your pardon. We are off the subject of your visit, Lady Blessingame. We should discuss the codicil to your late husband's will."

"Yes, and why wait two years to contact me?"

"That, my dear lady, was part of the terms of the will and its codicil. But that is my father's work, so we should hear from him. Father?" Richard Hargate said, turning toward his father.

Mr. Hargate senior rose from behind the desk. Standing, he was taller than Bella thought, judging by his hunched position when he sat at the desk. He turned to a dark, aged pinewood lawyer's cabinet behind him, the top a series of cubbyholes stuffed with papers bound with string. He pulled forward one or two packets of papers until he found the one he wanted. Untying the string that bound them, he sat at his desk again, unfolding the pages.

He resettled his glasses farther up on his nose. "Most unusual request; however, we have followed his instructions," he said, his voice raspy. He cleared his throat. "Lady Blessingame, what was listed in the original will you received was not the full extent of your inheritance from Sir Harry Blessingame. I was quite perturbed when he came to me. He acted like a man who did not expect to live long. When I protested that attitude, he forestalled me and merely said the work he did was dangerous, but vital, and he was a realist. I'd hoped, naturally, that he was wrong concerning his life expectancy; however, I followed his instructions."

"When did he come to you?" Bella asked.

"The week before you wed. He had everything planned out."

Bella and Gwinnie exchanged glances.

"Please continue, Mr. Hargate," Bella said.

"You have a house in Richmond."

"A house?"

"Yes. I gather at one time it was the abode of Sir Harry's female associates."

"His mistresses," Bella clarified.

"Er, yes. He'd arranged for the end of the last of

those associations and wanted the property rented
until two years after his death."

"Two years after his death?"

"Yes, those were part of his instructions. Then the
house was to be emptied of all existing furnishings,
chimneys swept, and the house modernized as
needed."

"Modernized in what way?" Bella asked.

"We had a coal chute installed to make coal de-
livery cleaner and easier, new coal stoves and heaters,
a couple of windows were replaced due to wood rot,
and an upstairs balcony railing repaired. If anyone
were to lean against it, they would have toppled to the
ground, so crumbled and rusty was the railing and its
footings. We updated the baths to today's standards,
and upgraded the kitchen ovens, scullery, and larders,
adding cupboards and tables. Oh, and there is a new
roof so the servants won't get rained on in their
quarters."

"It was in that bad a condition?"

"The tenants were not the best sort," Richard Hargate said, turning to scowl at his father.

"They had the funds," declared Hargate senior
garrulously.

"It must have cost a fortune! Where did the money
come from?" Bella asked. "The estate—as you know—
is barely above water. It could use an infusion of
money after what that beastly steward did to the property and the tenants. I have scrimped and saved all
year to make what repairs I could!"

Hargate senior grimaced. "I know. I have been
bound by the terms of your late husband's will. But
rest assured, you will have the funds now to outfit the
Richmond house as you like—which was Sir Harry's
intention—and to see to the repairs at Lennox Hill."

"How much are we talking about?" Bella asked.

"Six thousand pounds."

Bella's eyes widened. "That would certainly make a difference."

"Per annum," Richard Hargate added.

Bella and Gwinnie stared up at him. "Per annum?" Bella repeated, shocked.

"Yes, Lady Blessingame. Per annum."

"How?" Bella asked, looking between father and son.

"He developed the habit of saving and investing at a young age. He once told me one did not need to spend one hundred pounds to look as if one has spent that much. Then, during the Peninsular War, he not only gained his knighthood for his work, but was the recipient of prize money on numerous occasions. This was also invested."

"He had a sense of money. When I teased him about it once, he dramatically said: *I smell it*. And of course, we both laughed, but if what you say is true, he may have actually smelled money!" Bella said. Then she laughed.

The others looked at her.

"Harry always told Lord Candelstone he did not come from money, so if he wanted us to move in the social circles he desired us to move in, he had to pay for the appearances. And he did! We never paid for the fancy houses, the servants, the clothes we wore, none of it."

Richard Hargate nodded. "Our Harry lied. He came from money; however, he claimed none of it. He did gain money. Clever man."

"But I don't see how Uncle Candelstone did not know this," Gwinnie said. "Especially with the prize money."

"He probably just said he sent the money home without clarifying what 'home' meant."

"That is precisely what he did, Lady Blessingame, and if someone came around and questioned us, that was to be our answer as well. Home for Sir Harry meant his accounts here in England. No one asked the right questions."

"That is Harry," Bella said. She sat straighter in her chair and looked at Mr. Hargate senior. "So, I have a house that needs painting and furnishing, and I have funds. Where do we go from here?"

"We hired Jasper Gladely to see to the renovations," Mr. Hargate, the younger, said. "I would suggest you continue to work with him to complete your project. I have found him to be honest to a fault and talented with regards to homes. If you give me a day, I can arrange a meeting with him at the house in Richmond."

"That's the day of the ball," observed Gwinnie.

"Yes, that won't work," Bella agreed. "Can you try for three days hence?"

"I will certainly ask him and I'm sure he will be amenable."

"And how do I access my funds?"

"We have a letter for you to take to the bank. They will set you up appropriately," said Mr. Hargate, Senior.

"Perfect," she said, taking it from Mr. Hargate. "I thank you for your time."

"There is one more thing," the elder Hargate said. He got up and turned back to his lawyer hutch, and from the same cubbyhole he'd pulled out the will information, he pulled out another stack of papers tied in string. These he did not untie, but handed them to Bella across the desk.

"Sir Harry wanted you to have this correspondence. He told me it is what is in these letters that dictates the two-year waiting period before you receive all you deserve. He said they will anger and sadden you. And he hoped you could come to forgive him. He said, *I have always had the best of intentions for Isabella and my family. It just won't look that way, after my death.* Then he laughed, rather wryly, I thought."

Bella studied the packet of letters she held in her hand. It looked like five or six in total. She started to pull the string binding them.

Richard Hargate stayed her hand. "I would recommend you wait to look at those until you are in a place of peace and calm, and alone. Harry had been in a strange humor when he passed those over. He said to me before he left, *She will hate me,* and there was a slight sheen in his eyes. Then the corner of his mouth kicked up in that way of his, and the moment of honesty was gone. Based on that brief moment, I make my recommendation."

Bella looked down at the bundle she held, then nodded. "If these letters are as volatile as you fear, I should indeed need my space. Thank you. Gwinnie, shall we rescue your father's coachman from boredom?"

Gwinnie laughed, "Watts won't be bored. He makes friends wherever he goes. But we should be returning before Grandmother sets her favorite Bow Street Runner out to find us."

Bella thanked the gentlemen again, then descended the stairs to fetch Rose from her knitting and send a clerk for their carriage.

❧

BELLA THUMBED through the corners of the packet of letters she held in her lap as the carriage rattled over the cobblestone streets on their way back to Malmsby House. She frowned.

"What are you thinking?" Gwinnie asked softly.

"I recognize the hand of the author of these letters. Do you?"

"Should I?" Gwinnie asked.

Bella nodded slowly. "It is Lord Candelstone."

"Letters my uncle wrote to Sir Harry?"

"Yes. Letters Harry told the lawyers would make me angry and sad. Letters I had to wait two years after his death to read."

"That is curious," Gwinnie said. "Are you going to read them as soon as we get home?"

"Yes."

"I suggest you use my father's old study. It is near the nursery rooms." She smiled. "He liked to be near us when we were small. Now his study is near his bedroom. The old study is private, and you should not be disturbed—though I reserve the right to check on you," she said with a gentle smile. "I'll own I am curious about those letters as well, and we know my grandmother will be curious, too."

Her mouth twisted into contorted distaste. "Anything Uncle is involved in would be distasteful. I wish Aunt Catherine had married elsewhere; however, the two of them formed an attachment in childhood."

"So your grandmother told me. Thank you for the suggestion. I will use the old study if that is all right. Something tells me that being in my bedroom would make it worse."

Bella noticed Rose had stopped her knitting and was listening to them. It wouldn't do to have her affairs bruited about the servants' quarters. She stared back at Rose, letting the woman know with her glance and a slight shake of her head to be silent. She hoped she would.

Bella grasped the stack in both hands and sighed. She would know what this was about soon enough.

CHAPTER 4
THE LETTERS

Lady Malmsby insisted she learn all that had transpired at the lawyer's office. She was pleased to learn about Bella's income and the house. She voiced disappointment at how far out the house was from them. She then rallied and proclaimed it would be delightful to set up a house completely, deciding she would be part of the planning and execution, much to Bella's amusement. She also agreed the old study would be perfect and requested Mr. Harold to have tea sent up there.

Bella stopped in her bedroom to change, then made her way up the stairs, meeting the maid who'd brought up refreshments for her.

"Mr. Harold said to include one of the tarts Cook just took from the oven. They are still warm." She giggled. "And quite tasty, too," she confided.

Bella smiled at her. "Thank you. This looks perfect. Could you put it on that table there?" she asked, pointing to a round mahogany table in the center of the room.

"Yes, my lady. Would you care for me to pour?" the

maid asked after she set down the tea tray and its delights.

"No, that is quite all right," Bella told her.

After the maid curtsied and left the room, Bella poured herself tea, taking it and a warm tart to one of the wing chairs by the fireplace. She nibbled on the tart, knowing she was merely delaying the letters out of fear. The light from the windows negated the need for a lit lamp.

She brushed the crumbs from the tart off her lap and wiped the stickiness from her fingers before she finally picked up the small, dusty packet of letters and pulled the string loose. She stared at the packet.

There was a brief note on top of the letters addressed to her and in Harry's hand. She slowly unfolded it.

Isabella,

Please don't hate me. I asked you to marry me with the best of intentions. I admire you, and I couldn't imagine what Lord Candelstone would do otherwise, for he is determined to have you married within his little club of spies. I like to think that I am the best of a possibly bad lot of choices.

Harry

Bella set the note on the table beside her and slowly unfolded the first letter in the stack.

Sir Harry,

That Miss Melville is proving to be an invaluable asset, totally unlike her brother. Though I do need to commend the lad for recognizing her talent. And, of course, my meddlesome mother-in-law, the Duchess of Malmsby, for bringing her to my attention. Sometimes the old hag amazes me.

Who would have thought a young, naive girl would possess a natural talent in cryptography! She says it is a

*matter of searching the patterns. Whatever the root of her
brilliance, we need it.*

*You're not encumbered, and not likely to be, given your
carnal habits. I propose a marriage of convenience between
you and Miss Melville. She can accompany you and be on
hand to translate coded French missives. See to it.*

Candelstone

Lord Candelstone! Bella's brow furrowed. Why
should Lord Candelstone wish her to marry a British
spy?

Bella frowned at Candelstone's arrogance. She
didn't think even Harry would bow to that order. But
he had. Why?

Sir Harry,

What do you mean she is being courted by Nowlton?

*No, no, a thousand times no! Nowlton would never
allow her to help the war effort, or to work for me, for that
matter. My brother-in-law is a fussy prig. I have never understood how the two of you are friends.*

*You must break them apart. What is she thinking tying
herself to a gallery owner? She is too valuable a resource.*

Candelstone

Mr. Nowlton a fussy prig? Hardly.

At least Harry didn't jump to Candelstone's orders.
She put the letter aside and picked up the next one.
There was a pattern emerging that began pressing
heavily against her chest.

Sir Harry,

*She must not be allowed to marry Nowlton. You must
see that. It would be a disaster for us to lose her talent. Stop
this nonsense about Nowlton being your best friend since
school days. Leave childhood behind. There is a war on!
Napoleon must be defeated.*

*If you don't wish to marry her, I will find someone else
for her. She must be in our family of agents.*

Candelstone

It appeared Harry had had a modicum of loyalty to Nowlton. That pleased her. But Candelstone was wearing Harry down.

Sir Harry,

I have heard the rumors. Good job! One of your best talents, I think. So Nowlton believes she has been bedding others and has tried to dally with you. That will turn off our sanctimonious Nowlton. What are you telling Miss Melville? You have to do something on that side as well, as she might confront Nowlton and spoil the game.

I still think you should wed her. I'm considering Aldrich as her husband, but I had another plan for him. Nothing set in stone, so those plans could be changed.

Keep me informed. I am rubbing my hands with glee.

Candelstone

What?

Bella's mouth dropped open.

How could he? She silently cried out. And how could Aidan believe him?

Knowing Harry, she understood. He was so good at lies and rumors. Tears slid down her cheeks. She wondered if what she had been told had a crumb of truth, for Harry had ultimately done as Candelstone requested and spun a story for her as well, to drive a bigger wedge between them. Remembering herself back then, she didn't think she would have confronted Nowlton. She would have slunk away to hide. She closed her eyes as memories played in her mind. Yes, Harry had been very, very good.

Sir Harry,

Well played! Bravo! That bet in the book at White's was a stroke of genius. Nowlton seldom goes there, but all the young bucks do and read that book for wagers they can join and gossip about.

*No one will realize that the bet is in your hand and I
swear, after I got your last letter, I went to look at the book
myself. Your forgery of his signature was masterful. No one
would believe that wasn't Nowlton's. No woman wants to
be the subject of a gentleman's bet, and to say he will be
under her skirts before the season is out is masterful.*

*I'm fairly set on Lord Kasper, now, as her husband. Yes,
he is a bit of a reprobate, but it keeps her close.*

Candelstone

Lord Kasper! He is the worst of the worst! How
dare he assume he could so easily pull all our strings!

She sighed, her anger simmering. He dared because the truth was, he could.

There was one more letter.

Sir Harry,

*Congratulations on a job well done, and on your up-
coming nuptials. I'm pleased you could see the benefits of
marrying Miss Melville. She will be a tremendous asset to
us on the Continent with you. More so than if she remained
in England.*

*Yes, I agree. You will need to live the life associated with
wealth. You will be provided the means to do so. It is worth
it to have Miss Melville in our camp.*

*When is the wedding, and how soon can you sail for
Portugal?*

Candelstone

She set the last letter on the table with the others.
She stared at them. Poor Harry. She sighed. She wasn't
angry at him. Well, not totally. She understood him, so
it was hard to pull up the kind of anger that she
should feel. He was a Candelstone soldier, and he followed his commander. If anything, she was angrier at
herself for taking delight in solving coded messages. It
wasn't ladylike. Not that she could ever truly be ladylike, but still. And then to believe Harry's lies about

the bet in Whites! Of course, he'd arranged to have her brother see it and report to her it was there and in Nowlton's hand.

She lowered her head into her hands as gentle tears flowed for all she'd lost, for all that might have been. Yes, Harry treated her well, but she'd never loved him. She'd married him in wounded pride and he led her to a life far different that she'd ever imagined. Changed her. She was no longer the girl Aidan fell in love with, nor the girl who fell in love with him. So much time and so many circumstances had passed. Yes, she ached in her heart for Aidan, but the past was the past. She could not go back. Their opportunity for happiness lay behind them.

She cried until there were no more tears. She leaned her head back against the chair's cushions and stared blindly up at the ceiling. Oh, for life to have been different! But it wasn't. She had to go on from here. But how? Did she tell Aidan anything? She compressed her lips together tightly, her face puffy and hot from spent tears. *Oh Harry*, she whispered.

Sometime later, there was a knock on the study door. Bella roused herself. She must have fallen asleep. The room was dim now.

"Yes?" she called out.

The door opened slowly to Gwinnie and Lady Malmsby.

She smiled wanly at them. "I survived, as you can see. It was rough, as Harry warned, but I have survived and am ready to move forward with my life."

"Do you wish to talk about it?" Lady Malmsby asked.

"I would, but not now. I need to ponder all I've learned a bit more," she replied. She pointed to the letters on the table. "These were most insightful and explain much."

She laughed grimly. "At least I found out why Mr. Nowlton hates me," she said as she walked past Gwinnie and Lady Malmsby. "Everyone says Harry was an excellent actor and storyteller. I believe he outdid himself regarding Mr. Nowlton and me. Now I find myself exhausted and famished."

"Would you like a light repast sent to your room?"

Bella smiled. "That would be lovely."

Gwinnie looked at her anxiously. "Will you feel up to going to Lady Amblethorpe's Musicale this evening?"

"Where you will be playing?"

"Yes. I should like you to come. We have added a new member and a new instrument to our ensemble. A flute! It's amazing how the flute has added to what we are doing. Joaquín also plays the guitar."

"Joaquín. Is he Spanish? It seems all the Spanish play the guitar," Bella said.

Gwinnie grinned. "Yes, he is Spanish. I believe it is a popular instrument in that country, unlike the flute. But I tell you, Joaquín makes the flute sing. And to fall in love with his music is to fall in love with Joaquín."

"Was he that gentleman who walks with a limp who was with the group last week to practice?" Lady Malmsby asked.

"Yes. The limp is from a Peninsular War injury. He was lucky not to lose his leg."

"From what I could overhear coming from that room, he is good," Lady Malmsby said.

"I will come," Bella said. "However, I don't promise to be lively."

Gwinnie waved her hand dismissively. "It's a concert. You are not meant to be lively. You are meant to listen," she mock-scolded.

Bella laughed. "Quiet I can do." She turned to walk to her room.

Lady Malmsby gently laid a hand on her arm. "We will see you soon."

Bella smiled wanly and nodded.

LADY MALMSBY CAME out of the Lady Margaret Parlor just as Bella descended the stairs.

"There you are!" enthused Lady Malmsby. She raised an eyebrow at Bella's dark blue gown. "But we need to take you to the dressmakers and get you out of dark colors," she said severely. "I know you loved Sir Harry, but two years of mourning is enough."

"I didn't, you know," Bella said.

"Know what?"

"Love Harry. I admired him, respected him, and he could be fun. But I didn't love him," she said simply. "Where are the others?" she asked, to divert the conversation.

"Gwinnie left early to see the group is set up properly. I had Ann, her stepmother Mrs. Hallowell, and Ellinbourne go on ahead. I did not see any reason to seat five in a carriage."

"What about the Duke and Lord Lakehurst?" Bella asked. She'd only seen Lord Lakehurst at dinner the night before and the Duke at breakfast that morning.

"Arthur never comes to social events," Lady Malmsby said, so clearly exasperated with her eldest son that Bella laughed.

"Generally," she continued, her manner partially recovered, "Lake comes in his stead, but he says he needs to work on his next book as he promised it to his publisher at the end of the month and if he is going to take time off tomorrow night for Ann and Ellinbourne's ball, he has to write tonight."

"It bothers you that they aren't with us," Bella stated.

"Yes," said Lady Malmsby. She sighed. "But I don't know why it should, for they have ever been the same. Ann's is the first wedding we've had in many years and for that I am in a party mood and want everyone to join the festivities."

"They will. Tomorrow night."

"I know." She took her shawl from the waiting footman. "Thank you, Stephen," she said as she settled it around her shoulders.

Bella followed her to the carriage.

As the carriage pulled away from the curb, Bella turned to Lady Malmsby. "While we are here, alone, I'd like to tell you some of what was in the letters."

Lady Malmsby turned to her, her eyes shining in the dim carriage light, reflecting surprise and delight.

"The letters were from Lord Candelstone to Harry. I impressed Lord Candelstone with my cryptography skills."

"I knew he would be," Lady Malmsby said.

"He wanted me to work for the war effort."

"Which you were excited to do, I assume."

"Yes, but he didn't want me to be employed by him," Bella said carefully.

"What? How could you work and not be employed? Did he wish you to volunteer as you might to a charity?"

"No. He had another idea. He wanted me to marry one of his agents. To ensure access to me, I suppose.

He was convinced Mr. Nowlton would not want me working for him, should he and I marry."

Lady Malmsby considered the idea, then nodded. "That is likely true," she said. "Aidan does not care for his brother-in-law. He doesn't trust his methods, and by default, he doesn't trust him."

"With good reason," Bella told her. "In the letters, Lord Candelstone ordered Harry to marry me. Evidently, Harry did question that, as Nowlton was his best friend, and he knew Nowlton was courting me. I gleaned that from the letter Lord Candelstone wrote back. He told Harry the war effort was more important. He needed to end the direction of our suit and then to marry me himself. Which Harry quite brilliantly did, with neither Nowlton nor I the wiser. Remember those stories we believed about each other that I told you about yesterday? He played Nowlton and me like marionettes, with each turning from love to hate, though for me, it was more profound sorrow and betrayal."

Bella felt her eyes filling with tears again. This would never do. "Forgive me, I thought I could tell you all, but I find my emotions are too raw still."

"Dear God," murmured Lady Malmsby. "I knew I should have arranged to get him and Catherine sent to a diplomatic mission in Australia or Canada. They probably need spies there, too. But I thought Catherine could manage him. I thought she would manage him. Seems she has become as wrong-headed as he. My own daughter."

She laid her gloved hand on Bella's. "It's all right, my dear. You have said enough that I have an understanding that what occurred was not through anything you or Aidan did. Candelstone has ever been a thorn in my side since he was a child. I used to castigate myself for my uncharitable feelings toward him as he grew up, and it dismayed me when Catherine held a tendre for him from a young age. I never wanted to run the lives of my children; however, that is one relationship I should have wished otherwise."

"Please say nothing to Aidan, I mean Mr. Nowlton," Bella said.

"I'm glad you can still think of him as Aidan. I should have enjoyed having you as my daughter-in-law."

"And I should have enjoyed being your daughter-in-law."

"Perhaps now—"

"No, please don't even think that. I am not the young girl I was three years ago. I've seen and done much, much that I am ashamed to admit. Sometimes the guilt eats at me for what I learned to do and did for Harry and Lord Candelstone. No. That past has flowed by us."

Lady Malmsby squeezed her hand. "All right, but an old woman can hope. I should like to see Aidan happy with a wife and family of his own. He's become too aloof and formal. No longer the laughing boy who followed his older siblings about, eager to help with whatever they wished. He was adorable."

Bella laughed. "Well, that was certainly not a Nowlton I ever knew. But perhaps, when he learns the truth, as I have, he will be free to find love again."

❧

THE CROWD of carriages before the Amblethorpe house surprised Bella. "I've never seen a musicale so well attended," she said, as their carriage made its way to the front door.

"Yes," Lady Malmsby agreed, "But Lady Amblethorpe's are always well attended. You never know what might happen at one of these events. She had one last December for those who stayed in London over the holidays. It was crowded and during intermission Sir James and Lady Branstoke took the opportunity to request attendees to get their chimneys swept and be on the lookout for one little boy who had been kidnapped into the chimney sweep trade."

"Did their gambit work?"

"Would you believe it did?"

"And they rescued the child?"

"Yes. And that was perhaps the most bizarre occurrence, but there have been other events like breakups, apoplexies, robberies, horrendous performers. At first, these events dismayed Lady Amblethorpe. But it brought her attendees. She doesn't plan for odd things to happen, just sometimes they do. Gwinnie told me there might be another betrothal tonight," Lady Malmsby confided, as their carriage stopped before the Amblethorpe mansion and a footman opened their carriage door. "Someone asked for time during intermission."

"Ah!" Bella said. "That should be fun, then."

"Yes, indeed. But not a word to anyone," Lady Malmsby cautioned. She turned to accept the footman's hand to step out of the carriage.

Inside they made it quickly through the receiving line. Lady Amblethorpe, too pressed by those around her, could only acknowledge their presence in passing.

"The concert room is upstairs and to the right. It is really a ballroom; however, Lady Amblethorpe gives more musicales than she does balls. Let's see if we can find Ann, Mrs. Hallowell, and Ellinbourne. Or at least

Ann and Mrs. Hallowell. Ellinbourne is likely seated off to the side, sketching," Lady Malmsby said.

"Sketching?"

"Yes. He takes his sketchbook everywhere. I should ask him for a sketch of Gwinnie playing her violin. If he can capture the expression she gets on her face when she plays, that would be priceless to me."

At the top of the stairs, they found Ann and Mrs. Hallowell chatting with Lady Oakley and Mr. Rutherford.

"Where is Ellinbourne?" Bella couldn't help but ask, even though the Duchess had told her what he would be doing.

"He is at the end of the stairway overlook to the hall below, sketching. Said something about the vantage from there being an excellent exercise in perspective," Ann said.

"Shall we find seats, ladies—and Mr. Rutherford?" Lady Malmsby invited.

The group made their way into the music room. The Duchess shepherded them to an area of open seats.

"Do we save one for Ellinbourne?" Bella asked.

"Oh, no. He will be up and down the entire time, sketching from various angles," Ann said. "I have a stack of sketches he's done of me from all angles that I adore. I hope one time he will turn one or more into a painting. He's been talking about it."

Bella leaned closer to her. "Do you think he would do one of Gwinnie playing her violin? Lady Malmsby would love to have a sketch like that."

Ann nodded. "I'll go suggest it to him. I shall be right back," she whispered in return. She slipped out of her chair and made her way through the crowd of those entering the music room.

"Where did Ann go?" Lady Malmsby asked.

"To talk to her fiancé before the concert."

Lady Malmsby nodded. The musicians were coming toward the stage, finalizing their chair arrangement, flipping through sheet music.

Bella felt surprised and pleased to find the audience start to quiet at their appearance. She whispered as much to Lady Malmsby.

"Gwinnie and her performances are popular," Lady Malmsby whispered back.

Bella noted the manner Gwinnie displayed to the gentleman with a limp. An ensemble player took care of the gentleman's guitar case. She carried his flute case and arranged his music once at his seat. Though Bella could not hear Gwinnie's words, she appeared to speak to him solicitously.

Lady Malmsby had a sharp intake of breath. "Someone has finally captured Gwinnie's attention. But is he the right someone?" Lady Malmsby whispered softly into Bella's ear.

Bella shrugged. She was a stranger to the London society scene.

"I shall ask Nowlton to contact Mr. Martin," Lady Malmsby whispered.

Bella looked at her quizzically.

"Bow Street," she mouthed.

Bella's eyebrows rose.

Lady Malmsby shook her head. "Later," she murmured.

～

"THIS HAS BEEN A WONDERFUL CONCERT," Bella told Gwinnie during the intermission.

"I am glad you are enjoying it. I love giving con-

certs!" Gwinnie said, radiating excitement and joy.
"What did you think of our flutist? Isn't he fabulous?
He sounds professional to me; however, he swears he
is merely an amateur. He plays the guitar as well, but I
love his flute work so much I requested that be the instrument he primarily plays this evening, except for a
couple of folk pieces we will do after intermission."

"He is talented," Bella agreed.

"I've told him he can play the flute sitting, as
standing does tire him; however, he insists on standing. He says the flute sound can't sing if he is sitting."

"You are lucky to have met him."

"How did you meet him?" Lady Malmsby asked.

Gwinnie laughed. "At a music publisher, naturally.
That is where I have met most of my musician
friends."

"Who is he?" Lady Malmsby asked.

"Don Joaquín Pedroso y Castel," Gwinnie said.

"How has he come to be in England?"

"Business. He will be here through the summer, he
says. I wish we could keep him here longer. He is a
wonderful addition to our little ensemble." She tilted
her head to the side. "It would be better," she conceded, "if we had our pianoforte player at well. Unfortunately, he slipped and fell backward in some
excrement the street cleaning boy missed, and injured
his elbow, of all things."

"Gracious!" Bella said. "How unfortunate. Nonetheless, I think your group sounds perfect, even
without the pianoforte," Bella said.

Gwinnie smiled happily. "Thank you!" she said.
"Come, I'd like you to meet Don Pedroso y Castel. You
will like him. He is such a personable fellow, and has
such exquisite manners!" she proclaimed.

Bella and Lady Malmsby exchanged quick glances.

Bella knew Lady Malmsby was concerned for Gwinnie's enthusiasm, but she merely told her granddaughter they would be delighted to meet the gentleman.

Gwinnie led them to an antechamber just beyond the concert room.

"I thought you said there was to be a betrothal during intermission."

Gwinnie laughed as they walked. "There was supposed to be—however, the intended fiancé has fled the city with another man!"

"So much for Lady Amblethorpe's odd happening at her concert," Lady Malmsby said.

"Oh, I don't know. I'm sure the story will get around of what was supposed to happen that didn't. That will set the gossips' tongues, don't you think?" Gwinnie said.

"Hmm, perhaps that's true," Lady Malmsby conceded. "Can't have Lady Amblethorpe's concert marred by a lack of excitement."

Bella and Gwinnie laughed.

"Don," Gwinnie said, as they entered the room where the musicians were sitting and enjoying refreshments, "I'd like you to meet my grandmother, the Duchess of Malmsby."

The gentleman rose slowly, relying lightly on a cane, and bowed deeply. "I am grateful to make the acquaintance of a personage such as yourself, your grace," he said. His voice was deep, and a little husky.

After her time working for Candelstone, Bella studied the Spaniard before her. He sported a trimmed beard with a waxed, twirled mustache. Curious—it appeared he resorted to a touch of blacking for his hair and beard. The vanity of some men, she thought as she smiled to herself.

When he and the Duchess had finished their greeting, Gwinnie introduced her. "This is our friend, Lady Blessingame, from Derbyshire."

"Enchanted, Lady Blessingame," the man said with his slight Spanish accent, as he bent over her hand, holding it a moment longer than necessary.

"I quite enjoyed your flute playing," she told him.

"Thank you, you are all graciousness to a mere amateur musician as myself," he said, placing his hand on his chest.

Bella stepped back as she silently acknowledged his words. She didn't know why, but the man made her uncomfortable. She felt like he was silently laughing at her, and she could not conceive why.

"We will see you again after the concert," Lady Malmsby told Gwinnie.

They left Gwinnie with her musician friends and went in search of Ann and Ellinbourne.

"I did not like him," Bella said softly to Lady Malmsby.

"Why? He seemed like any other of the parade of gentlemen who've decided they'd like to capture the interest of a duke's daughter," Lady Malmsby said drily.

"Yes, I can see that," Bella said. "But there was something else. Like he was laughing at me—or at us," she exclaimed, her brow furrowing as she thought of the gentleman. "You grace, why hasn't Gwinnie ever married?"

"After her mother died, her passion turned from music to food, and she became quite ample and therefore, terribly shy. Since my son Arthur does not socialize much, it was easy for her to stay away from social functions. Thankfully, music once again reclaimed its hold on her, and she sometimes just forgets to eat. She has slimmed down, but now lacks interest in marriage. At seven-and-twenty, she considers herself on the shelf."

"I am sure there are men who would not hold her spinster status against her."

"Yes, but she also feels they only overlook it for her position in society. She is confident as a musician—she is not confident as a woman. It is a bit of a conundrum, you see.—Oh, there are Ann and Ellinbourne. Ann is looking through his sketchbook. He must have been quite busy! I wonder if he'll show us," she said.

They made their way to the back of the concert room.

"Have you done many sketches, Ellinbourne?" Lady Malmsby asked.

"Many!" said Ann excitedly. "And they are wonderful! Here, let me show you this one of Gwinnie," she said, as she flipped back through the book. "Here!" She handed the sketch over to Lady Malmsby.

"Ah!" Lady Malmsby's breath caught. "It is stunning." Her eyes watered. "You have so caught her emotion, her feeling for the music, and this is only a sketch!" she said. She looked up at Ellinbourne, a lone tear sliding down her cheek. "How do you do it? I wish she saw herself like this; however, if she sees this sketch, I doubt she will see what I see."

Ann handed her a handkerchief while Bella gently took the sketchbook from her hand.

The Duchess dabbed at her cheeks. "Thank you, Ann. Silly, me. I don't know why this sketch catches at me so powerfully. Can you—can you do this in paints?" she asked tentatively.

Ellinbourne nodded solemnly.

"I have a suggestion for this, too, that would touch Gwinnie's heart, your grace," Bella said to Lady

Malmsby. She turned to Ellinbourne. "You, your grace," Bella said, addressing Ellinbourne, "you should name a price that a portrait painter would charge. And then the Duchess can pay that sum to the charity Gwinnie helps with."

Lady Malmsby brightened. "I like that idea."

Ellinbourne laughed shortly. "I have never sold a painting. I have no idea what to charge."

"Never sold? That's outrageous!" Lady Malmsby said. "You should sell your works, even if you donate the money to charity. And as for a price, Aidan would know to the penny what it is worth."

Bella flipped through the sketchbook as Ann had done. There was another sketch of Gwinnie from another angle, though it did not have the same power of emotion as the first. She flipped another page to a quick sketch of the ensemble. She stopped on a sketch of Don Pedroso y Castel. Ellinbourne caught that gentleman's love of his music, as well. But for some reason Bella couldn't articulate, she did not like the gentleman. Perhaps because she suspected he was planning to swindle, steal, or otherwise break Gwinnie's heart. Bella vowed to be vigilant.

The musicians reentered the room and resumed their places. Lady Malmsby, Bella, and Ann returned to their seats, leaving Ellinbourne to his prowling the floor for the best artistic prospects.

He really was quite talented, Bella thought. Pity he was a duke.

CHAPTER 5

THE BETROTHAL BALL

Bella knocked softly on Ann's door. Her maid opened it.

"Ann, may I come in? May I see?" Bella asked.

She heard Ann laugh as she peered around the maid.

"Yes! Of course. Grandmother and Gwinnie are here before you."

Bella stepped into Ann's bedroom. "Oh! You're beautiful!" she said, as she eyed the pale blue and soft green creation with its foam of white tulle neckline glittering with paste gems sprinkled on it. With her honey-gold hair, Ann looked like a mythical mermaid rising out of the sea. "Is that a Madam Vaussard creation?" she asked.

"Yes," Lady Malmsby said.

"How did Madam Vaussard come by such beautiful fabric? It looks like the ocean shimmering, changing from blue to green as she moves with the light."

"It's from a sari," Gwinnie enthused. "Madam Vaussard traded an Indian woman one of her ready-made day dresses for the sari. There was enough fabric in the sari for two over-dresses, so she made out well in that transaction," she said with a grin.

"Definitely. I had heard she was a shrewd businesswoman."

Lady Malmsby nodded. "Oh, she is. But what is this with you? You're still wearing half-mourning?"

Bella shrugged, "I have not visited the modistes in London yet. This was my best ball gown when I was in Brussels last year."

Lady Malmsby frowned. "I thought—all society thought—Sir Harry was swimming in funds."

Bella sighed. "The estate Harry inherited from his mother, and was given to me as part of the marriage settlement, has been terribly mismanaged. The old steward was bleeding it dry while we were gone. More money going into his own pockets than into the estate. I have hired a new steward. We are investing into the estate this year. Unfortunately, the unusually cold Spring has not helped the tenants recover, either. The steward and I are setting budgets and goals."

Lady Malmsby nodded. "Commendable. Still, you need to look swimming in funds even if you aren't. We can help with that," Lady Malmsby said, signifying herself, Ann, and Gwinnie. "For as gorgeous as your half-mourning ball gown may be, particularly with that exquisite Brussels lace ornamentation, you need to be in colors," stated Lady Malmsby flatly.

Bella laughed at the Duchess's manner. "You should have been one of the commanders in the military."

"I don't deny that," Lady Malmsby said airily. "If women had been, the war would not have lasted as long as it did."

Gwinnie started giggling. "I can just imagine the patronesses of Almack's in command."

Bella blinked, then a grin slowly changed her expression to glee. "I suddenly have an image in my mind of Lady Jersey before the enemy, talking fast and furiously as she stares them down," she said.

The ladies all laughed, then Lady Malmsby dismissed them to go downstairs before the guests began to arrive.

～

THE BETROTHAL BALL for Ann and the Earl of Ellinbourne was a crushing success, as Aidan had been certain it would be—his mother did nothing in moderation.

Despite the crowd, Aidan spotted Lady Blessingame shortly after he had arrived. His expression hardened when he saw she still wore half-mourning for Harry. Made his stomach churn. Had she'd loved the churl that much? How could he have been so wrong about her three years ago! All he knew then of her was her sweetness and a lively, fun intelligence. He never would have imagined she hid a wanton trollop behind the mask she wore in front of him. That made her as good an actor and liar as Harry.

He had asked the same question over and over in the intervening years, and still had no answers, and still the pain of her betrayal lingered.

She moved elegantly, no longer displaying the exuberant bounce of youth that he well remembered. She greeted those she knew with warmth and welcomed introductions to those she didn't know with a graceful smile. The guests represented the best of society; however, the subdued, elegant gown she wore made her stand out all the more in the glittering throng around her. All the easier to avoid her, he sourly thought.

He lounged against one of the white alabaster columns that rimmed the ballroom and watched her. Oh yes, she was still quite the dissembler.

The only time he saw her discomfited was when Lord Candelstone came near her. It appeared she purposely slid around a large fern to the back shadows of the alabaster column near where she'd stood.

When Candelstone passed on, she came out from hiding, her expression cold.

That was interesting to observe.

The next moment, a young buck came up to talk to her, and she was all smiles and laughter once again.

BELLA SAW Mr. Nowlton watching her.

The laughter and smiles she bequeathed to those around her grew louder and brighter. She would not allow Nowlton to spoil her enjoyment of the ball. This was an event for dear Ann and the Duke of Ellinbourne. Nowlton's sour disposition did not belong here, and she would not allow him to lead her to the same attitude.

She sighed as she risked another glance in his direction. She did not want him to know she'd noticed him. But he looked quite handsome standing over to the side of the room, in a pose of casual elegance, as he studied the crowd of guests and watched her.

"Oh, Aidan," she whispered to herself.

The Marquess of Sherringvale's son came up to solicit her for the next dance. She couldn't remember the young man's name; however, she smiled brightly at him and let him lead her into the line forming for a country dance.

After the exuberant dance, Bella stood alone, fanning herself, while her dance partner left to fetch a glass of cooling punch.

"He watches you, you know," came Lord Candelstone's voice from behind her left shoulder.

She whirled around to confront him. Her mistake had been in not returning to her position near the wall, preventing surprise encounters. Harry would have reprimanded her for that.

"What do you want?" she demanded.

"You need to come back to work for me," he said.

"The war is over, Lord Candelstone. I am retired."

He snorted. "Wars abound, threatening the fabric of our society."

She frowned at him and started to turn away.

He laid a gloved hand on her forearm to stop her.

She looked down at his hand.

"There are terrorists in this country," he continued, "who communicate amongst each other in code. We need you to decipher their communications so we can route these traitors out."

"No." She pushed his hand off her arm. "Leave me alone."

"I cannot do that, Lady Blessingame. You owe service to the country."

Anger flared white hot. "I don't owe you or the country anything!" she hissed. "Harry saved those letters you sent to him three years ago. The letters where you ordered him to destroy my happiness."

He did not pretend to not understand her. "Happiness with Nowlton? I saved you from him! You should thank me," he boasted.

Her former dance partner came up beside her

with two glasses of punch, avidly listening to her ex-
change with Candelstone.

Bella turned to him. "Ah, my punch. Thank you,"
she said, forcibly modulating her voice as she smiled
up at him, her eyes glistening with emotion. "Shall we
drink our punch while we take a turn about the
room?" she suggested, not giving the young man a
choice as she took the punch glass in one hand and
threaded her other arm through his. She turned him
away from Candelstone. The young man easily followed where she led.

"We are not done yet, Lady Blessingame," Candelstone said, *sotto voce*.

Still, Bella heard him and shivered slightly.

BELLA SAW Nowlton's lips curl as she and her partner
passed on their perambulation about the room.

Aidan Nowlton and Lord Candelstone. They were
vining thorns wrapped about her, scratching her,
drawing pinpricks of blood with every move she
made. They drained her vitality. It was early in the
evening, and she felt incredibly tired. She would be
missed if she retired to her room, so she couldn't do
that. There would be more questions.

She sighed. Always questions.

Suddenly, she stopped. She dropped the young
man's arm. "Would you excuse me, please? There is
something I must do," she told him. She handed her
half-full punch glass back to the confused young man
and made her way back around the room to where
Nowlton stood, watching.

He looked at her in surprise when she stopped in
front of him.

"I wish to speak with you," she said.

He looked at her through hooded eyes. "I have nothing to say to you."

"That is fine. You don't need to talk. You need to listen," she said grimly. She grabbed his arm and pulled him away from the column he leaned against. "Come, the column will stand without your support."

Around her, she heard a sudden burst of whispers and saw curious faces. Gossips. She ignored them.

"This is not wise," Nowlton said as she led him through the room.

"On the contrary, this is the wisest thing I've done since coming to London. This way..."

She led him to the Duke's old study on the same floor. She pulled him inside and shut the door behind them.

She turned around to face him. A racehorse couldn't gallop faster than her heart beat. She licked her lips. "First, let me say," she began carefully, "I never bedded Harry or any other man before I married."

Nowlton snorted. "That is not what I know. But why do you persist in this lie? It has been three years!"

"No! We were lied to!" She took a deep breath. "It all comes back to Harry. Our charming Harry was incapable of loving anyone, but he loved to be loved. He loved to be appreciated, to receive praise. He hated criticism of any kind."

Aidan's mouth compressed in a straight line, but he conceded that was Harry's biggest fault. His brows pulled together. "But why are you mentioning this?" he quizzed.

Bella sighed. "Harry would do what he had to do to receive love, admiration, respect, all of those feel-good feelings. And if that was acting in love, or doing things he didn't want to do, he would do that. But emotionally, he was empty. The only way he felt fulfilled was if others loved and admired him. He fed off of that love, but he didn't reciprocate."

"Did you love him?"

"I tried to. He feigned such love for me while my heart was broken. I couldn't refuse. I really didn't care who I wed when you rejected me."

"What are you talking about? That is the second time you have intimated that I somehow hurt you when it was you who hurt me. You are playing with me again. I should know that once a game-playing spy, always a game-playing spy."

He turned to walk away. She grabbed his arm.

"It's time you stop wearing your hurt on your sleeve and listen to me!" she entreated. "We were both deceived, and we played right into Harry's plan."

"You are wrong. Harry and I were good friends."

"If you were such good friends, why did Harry tell me you had a bet on the books at White's that you would be under my skirts before the season was out?"

"What?! No, that is not Harry!"

"It is when he is under orders from your brother-in-law," she hissed.

"Candelstone? What fairy tales are you promoting now?"

Bella compressed her lips a moment and glared at him. Then she relaxed and sighed. "If you will hear me out," she said, striving for a calmer, slower voice, "I will tell you what I only discovered yesterday about your presumably best friend—my husband—and your so-illustrious brother-in-law, Lord Candelstone."

He raised an eyebrow in doubt but gave a slight nod.

She paused a moment. Wondering how to begin.

"Might we sit?" she asked.

He reluctantly nodded. He picked up the oil lamp from the round table in the center of the room and brought it over to the pair of wing chairs facing each other in front of the cold fireplace. The same place she'd sat the other day.

She spied her packet of letters on the table between the chairs. She thought she had carried it back to her room. If Nowlton still required proof, it would be this.

Aidan placed the lamp on the mantel. In the background, they heard the sounds of the ball, laughter and music—a world away—as they settled in a pool of dim light across from each other.

Aidan tried to look at her dispassionately, to put aside the hurts he'd harbored for three years. It was only after seeing her again that he realized he hadn't recovered from the way things ended between them. He thought he had moved on with his life; however, he saw now that was a sham thought.

Though the lantern light might be dim, he could see the difference between his memories of Bella and the woman who sat across from him. The Bella he remembered loved to laugh, for she truly loved life and all it could offer. This woman appeared reserved, withdrawn from life, looking all about for danger. She moved with grace and assurance, none of the bounce in her step and excitement in her manner that Aidan remembered of the smart young minx he'd become enamored with. This woman appeared to have been drained of any joy.

He watched her hands move restlessly as she spoke.

"When I returned to England from Brussels when the war ended," she said softly, "I retired to Lennox

Hill. Not long ago, I received a summons from Harry's solicitor requesting my presence in London. He said there was remaining business concerning the will that needed to be communicated. I preferred to do our business through the mails, as I enjoyed my solitary life, but the solicitor was insistent. At the time, Lord Candelstone was also importuning me to come back to work for him. And he wouldn't stop. I wanted to tell him in person the answer was a firm, *No*. So, with both pending tasks before me, and with my brother stationed here, I came to London.

"Yesterday, Gwinnie and her maid accompanied me to Harry's solicitor's office. Hargate, Owen, and Hargate."

"I am slightly familiar with them," Aidan said.

Bella nodded. "Harry had written a codicil to the will that was not to be read until two years after his passing. The codicil gave me the rest of his estate. I didn't know there was anything else to his estate. He kept it secret. The codicil included a house in Richmond and a generous annuity. Fairly straightforward as inheritances go, save for the two-year wait time."

"So, what is your point? What has this to do with what happened three years ago?" Aidan impatiently asked. He didn't want to be this near to her. She brought up too many memories, and not all of them terrible memories. Some memories set off a yearning in his chest.

She nodded, her head cocked to the side. "I'm getting to that." She took a deep breath. *Would he believe her? Would it matter if he did or didn't?*

"Before I left the solicitor's office, he gave me a packet of letters that Harry also told them not to deliver until the same two years had passed."

She looked at the packet of papers on the small

table. "These are the letters the solicitor gave me," she said, poking at the stack. "They were exceedingly enlightening. Since I read them, I have alternated between hysterical tears and hysterical laughter. But I will say one thing: Harry was a master at long-range planning. Read them," she invited.

"I will read nothing from Harry, that double-crossing fake friend."

One corner of Bella's mouth quirked upward in a wry half smile. "He wasn't as much of a fake friend as you think. His own need for love and admiration conflicted. Please read them."

"No!"

"Are you afraid?"

"Of course not."

"Then stop the theatrics and read them. Now, while we sit here. I dare you."

He scowled at her. "Are you threatening me?" he asked.

She rolled her eyes. "Really? Please, as a favor to me, and to your mother, who is familiar with the contents of the letters, read them."

"Lady Malmsby has read these letters?" he asked.

"No, but I told her about them, and the gist of their contents."

He frowned but nodded.

He read the first note. "That is an odd letter from Harry."

"I know. Read on and you will understand more."

"What?" he suddenly said, holding one page out in front of him. "Why should Candelstone care whom we marry?"

"Not you," she said, pointing at him. She turned her pointing gesture toward herself. "Me."

"I don't understand."

"He wanted me to work for the War Office, deciphering coded messages. But he wouldn't hire me. He decided it would be better if I were married to someone who was already associated with the War Office."

"Harry," Aidan said.

"Yes. But Harry wasn't keen to the idea, for in the next letter from Candelstone, he acknowledged that, but pressured Harry to do what he could do to break up our relationship, to give Candelstone time to find someone else in the War Office who would marry me!"

He frowned, looked back at the letters he held and began to read again.

Bella leaned back in her chair and stared up at the ceiling. "When I read that letter, I cried. I had never felt so used... and useless in my entire life," she said as he read.

She looked back at Aidan. "To learn someone could think so little of me. I mean, I know I am not a beauty; however, I am not ill- favored. And I was not an heiress, but not totally penniless, either. I don't believe Harry liked the choices Candelstone named as husband for me. Does that show a slight bit of care? I don't know. But I like to think that is why Harry finally told him he would marry me."

"With Lord Kasper suggested, I would like to think even that match would prick what little conscious Harry had."

"Perhaps. Candelstone's last letter in the stack was a congratulatory letter for a job well done. He told Harry he would have a valuable asset in me. It was an excellent decision to marry me. Tidied things up nicely, and how soon before we could leave for Portugal?"

"Harry was like a brother to me," Aidan said. "He knew how I felt about you. He was the only one who knew. Ultimately, that didn't matter." He stopped with a deprecating laugh. He shook his head. "You know, I don't know what is worse. The betrayal I felt from you three years ago or the betrayal I feel now from Harry."

Bella nodded. "I understand, I really do. If it is any consolation, I have the same conundrum. Storytelling to both of us. About that bet on the books at White's... that crushed me. He said he knew it would, and offered me his shoulder to cry on. Which I did. He was so gentle and kind to me in those early days. So sorry for what his good friend was planning. He had to tell me."

"But how could you have so little faith in me? I thought you knew me better than that!"

"I could say the same of you! Me with wanton behavior? I was so young and naïve I didn't even know what wanton behavior was! Harry reminded me you were the youngest of the Nowltons and inherited little from the old Duke, your father, and that as a consequence, you needed a wife with funds. You couldn't afford to marry me. He said, quite sadly for me, you were playing with me."

Aidan nodded. "An odd use of truth and lies," he said grimly. "I did not inherit from my father. That is true. However, Harry knew I had inherited money from my grandmother, Lady Margaret Sudbury. I did not, and do not, need an heiress for a wife. But why did you marry him?"

"He asked," she said simply. "I was so depressed. If someone had suggested I jump in the Thames, I might have."

"No!" Aidan looked at her helplessly. He'd spent years thinking the worst of her, at times hating her. He had a hard time getting his mind around these revelations. To be the author of such misery for her because of his lack of faith shook him.

"I'm really quite foggy in my mind about that time," Bella continued.

She exhaled deeply and stared off; her gaze was unfocused when she spoke again. "I felt punched in the stomach and breathless. I went on with life like a wound-up music box, pasting a smile on my face and doing the twirling motions of the same dance over and over and over again," she softly said. "And his promise of leaving England sounded so welcome right then."

She looked at Aidan then as she smiled wryly. "When Harry turns on the charm, he is hard to resist. He drew both men and women to him and they clamored to be his friend."

Aidan shook his head. "Everyone except my mother. I should have paid more attention to her observations. I wouldn't say she didn't like him," he said consideringly. "That might be too strong. However, she never trusted him, and felt it fitting he would work for Silly Willy, as she sometimes called Candelstone. I suppose I was one of those charmed. I wonder what he wanted from me?"

"Connections," Bella said flatly.

"Connections?"

She nodded. "Yes, Harry once told me, in one of his odd fits of confidences, that his family had money; however, they were reclusive, and he didn't have the opportunity to meet people until he went to school. That is when he realized there was a world beyond his family's estate and the village nearby. His family did not socialize. He continued to be oddly bitter about that, though he was a center of any social group."

The door to the Duke's study opened. "Finally, I've found you. What are you doing in here?" demanded Captain Andrew Melville, striding into the room.

"Talking," replied Bella. She glared at her brother.

"But you are in here alone. With him," protested Captain Melville.

"Yes. And?" Bella asked, outraged.

"You'll be ruined!"

Bella relaxed as she laughed. "Andrew, I am not a young debutante. I am a widow."

"Still, it is not seemly. If anyone but me had walked in—"

"And what would they have seen? Two people making mad, passionate love on the study floor?" Bella asked sarcastically.

Aidan looked at her in surprise, slowly realizing the woman who sat across from him was not the woman he knew three years ago. He didn't know how he felt about that.

"And how is it that you came in here?" Aidan asked. "My brother's study is not near the festivities."

"Lord Candelstone asked me—"

Bella exploded out of her chair and flew at Andrew, shoving him backward a step.

Aidan surged to his feet.

"I told you to never say his name to me!" Bella yelled at Andrew. She pushed her brother again. "And what are you doing talking to him?"

She would have shoved him again, but Andrew caught her arms before she could touch him.

"Bella! He was concerned for you. He saw you walk off with Nowlton. After your history—"

"Aargh!" she cried. She pulled loose from Andrew's grip and turned to Aidan. "He's doing it again! He won't leave me alone!"

She threw herself back into her chair as she burst into tears.

"Did she really ask you not to say his name again?" Aidan asked Captain Melville.

"Yes, but—"

"You are a fool, Melville," Aidan said harshly. He turned toward Bella and squatted down by her chair. "And so am I," he whispered. He pressed his handkerchief into her hands.

Happiness pushed aside for *King and Country*. Candelstone's favorite phrase to justify his actions. But why would his brother-in-law care now what Bella did, or who she talked to? He rose to his feet to face Melville.

"Where's Candelstone?

"When I left him, he said he was going to speak to Ann and Ellinbourne, to personally offer his congratulations on their engagement."

Aidan nodded. "Stay here with her until I can send my mother, the Duchess, or my niece Gwinnie to her. Do not talk to her or explain yourself. Just leave her alone."

"But I can explain."

"Later, you can explain to me. Leave her alone. You don't understand the magnitude of what she has lived through, and what truths she discovered yesterday." Aidan knew he did not understand the magnitude of her experiences either, and he had been a small part of them.

He laid a hand on Melville's shoulder. "It would be a kindness to her for you to leave her alone right now," he finished.

Melville looked from him to her and reluctantly agreed.

CHAPTER 6
THE TERRACE

Aidan scanned the ballroom for Candelstone. He didn't know what he would say to the man. He just knew Candelstone had a truly evil, Machiavellian mind, hiding behind a veneer of civility. How could he treat people as pawn chess pieces, to be moved around and sacrificed as needed to realize goals? It was untenable. And for his own sister to be married to him! Aidan considered it fortunate they'd never had any children. He would see that he never bothered Lady Blessingame again. He didn't know how, but that woman deserved peace.

He could not find Lord Candelstone; however, he spied his sister, Catherine, with a small knot of London society matrons. The gossip set. He made his way over to them. He smiled and bowed to them as a group.

"Ladies, pardon this intrusion," he said, clasping his hands together while he slightly bowed to them. "If you would not mind, I should like a brief word with my sister," he said, nodding at Lady Catherine Candelstone.

"Of course, Aidan!" his sister said, coming to his side as the other ladies tittered their agreement.

He drew Catherine off a few feet away from the others. "Where is Candelstone?" he asked, as he continued to peruse the room.

"William has gone to the card room with mother and Lady Oakley. I think she means to try to fleece him," she laughed. "Slight chance of that. Why do you ask?"

Aidan fixed his gaze on her face. "Did you know he arranged for Sir Harry Blessingame to do whatever was needful to end my courtship of Miss Melville?"

"Yes—Oh, not at that time," she blurted, when she saw fury build in her brother's face. "I only learned of it—quite accidentally from Candelstone—after Sir Harry's death. He muttered now he needed to find another handler for Bella."

"*Handler?*"

She nodded, unaware of how ominous that word sounded to Aidan. "I queried him on this statement, even if I wasn't supposed to hear it. Though he was reluctant, I pressed him, and I learned the story. It is astonishing Harry could do that."

"Why didn't you tell me?"

"What would have been the point? That was over three years ago."

He sighed as he shook his head. "Catherine, it would have been a kindness to both of us if you had. I have held a hatred for her for three years."

"Oh no, Aidan, surely not hatred. That is a strong word," she protested.

"Unfortunately, it is the right word. If you will excuse me, I would speak with him."

"What are you planning, Aidan?" she asked, now worried.

"I'm not sure yet. If he isn't with Mother, I will punch him out or challenge him to a duel, or both. Consider him lucky if he is with Mother," he said as he walked away.

He found Gwinnie speaking to the musicians. Hardly surprising for his musical niece.

"A moment, Gwinnie?" he asked. "Lady Blessington has had a trying evening. I left her in Malmsby's old study with her brother, whom I ordered not to talk to her. But I think she needs someone with her who is not likely to call forth potent emotions. Can you go to her?"

"What happened? Did you berate her?" she accused, hands on her hips as she glowered at him.

He shook his head. "I wanted to, and tried, but she berated me instead. Rightly so. We have been living in a tangled web created by Lord Candelstone, whom I am looking for right now. He needs to leave her alone."

Gwinnie relaxed. "I won't pretend to understand, but I shall certainly go to her. I like Bella."

"Thank you."

Satisfied, Aidan quickly descended two flights of stairs to the ground floor and turned right toward the formal parlor. Just beyond that was the sitting room set up as a card room, or a music room, as needed. Only his mother used the ground floor Lady Margaret Parlor across the hall. She'd ordered it closed to guests, and no light leaked around the door frame.

He stood in the card room's doorway for a moment. It appeared his mother's table was finishing a set. Judging by her expression, she and Lady Oakley won. Candelstone scowled at the gentleman who sat as his partner. Aidan smiled. His mother could count cards with the best of the card sharks.

He walked toward their table.

"Aidan!" his mother called out when she saw him approach. "Come join us! Mr. Rutherford wants to cry off another game. I'm just getting warmed up."

"I'll bet you are," Aidan said drily. "No, I'm not here to play," he said, laying a hand on Mr. Rutherford's shoulder to forestall him getting up. "I'm here to speak to Candelstone," he said.

Candelstone leaned back in his chair, draping an arm across the low back. "Yes?" he said. "You look like you have eaten something disagreeable, Nowlton."

"I have a warning for you," Aidan said. "Leave Lady Blessingame alone."

Candelstone snorted. "Or what? I have only her best interests at heart."

Lady Malmsby laughed. "Now that is a bounder."

"Stay away from her," Aidan warned, his voice louder than he intended. He noted several heads turned in their direction. He ground his teeth.

"What? Are you thinking of courting her again?" Candelstone mockingly asked.

Aidan shook his head. "We have gone our separate ways, but I won't see her hurt again. She has been through too much due to you."

Candelstone laughed harshly, his lips curling at the corner. "Looks like Blessingame taught her well. She's an asset to the country."

Aidan's eyes narrowed. He wanted nothing more than to grab the man by his lapels and slam him against the wall. Only the knowledge that would bring more distressing rumors down on Lady Blessingame stopped him.

Lady Malmsby rapped Candelstone's arm with her fan. "Candelstone, you are supposed to be retired," she said severely. "It's time you stopped playing spymaster. Leave that poor woman alone, or I shall see they send you to some inhospitable government outpost—and you know I can do so," Lady Malmsby warned.

Lady Oakley nodded agreement.

Whispers rose throughout the room following the Duchess's statement.

Candelstone straightened around in his chair and leaned forward. "No one is above our King and our country," he hissed at Lady Malmsby.

Lady Malmsby compressed her lips as she snorted. She turned to look across the table at Lady Oakley. "Sally, I believe it is your deal."

Aidan dropped his staying hand from Mr. Rutherford's shoulder. He nodded toward his mother and Lady Oakley, then turned to leave the room.

Satisfied with the results of the encounter with his brother-in-law, Aidan smiled.

BELLA LEANED her head back in the wing chair, her eyes closed. Before journeying to London, she hadn't cried in a long while. Hadn't allowed herself to. Now in two days she was making up for forfeited tears. Her brother's betrayal hit her hard. Andrew wasn't an unintelligent man, he simply lacked sensibility. Unfortunately, Lord Candelstone had early in their association learned to make use of this gap in her dear brother's personality.

She opened her eyes. Her brother sat across the room, leaning forward, his head down, elbows resting on his knees and his hands dangling between his legs.

He must have felt her regard, for he looked up then, his expression one of dejection. They looked much alike save for his blond hair to her dark brown hair. Both had firm chins, which on him lent him a masculine beauty that on her took away any pretense of feminine beauty. Thinking of her appearance, she wondered what Aidan Nowlton had ever seen in her to draw his admiration. He was a man who lived with beauty every day with the paintings and other art pieces in his gallery. Perhaps that is why he could believe the lies Harry wove.

She sighed. Best not to think of that time. It was the past, and like the water flowing down the Thames, it had vanished in the fullness of time into the vastness of the ocean.

"Bella," her brother plaintively said.

She shook her head. "No Andrew. Don't speak."

"But I—"

"No!" Bella asserted. She rose from the chair. "Don't." She walked toward the door.

"Where are you going," Andrew asked, rising to his feet as well.

"For a walk in the garden."

"I'll come with you!" he said eagerly.

"No. I wish to be alone, to allow the coolness of the evening to soothe my heated countenance," she tossed out with dramatic mockery. "Allow me that."

Her brother shifted from one foot to the other. "If you are certain..."

"I am certain," Bella said. She opened the door. "Go enjoy the ball. Dance with a young lady or two. Perhaps you'll find your love," she said whimsically, as she smiled gently at him.

Bella descended the back servants' stairs to avoid seeing anyone—especially Aidan Nowlton. She didn't know how she felt about him now, in the fullness of knowledge as to how they both were deceived and manipulated.

Her tears belonged to the girl she had been. Strange they should come now. That girl no longer existed. She had seen too much, done too much, lived in a world of deceit for so long that truth and lies blended together. Loyalty to a mission trumped loyalty to people. In retrospect, she saw she'd grown callous.

She pushed down on the handle of the glass-fronted door leading to the terrace. With the London ballroom near the top of the mansion, few people descended the stairs to walk the terrace and garden.

A slight damp chill hung in the air, not as cold as most of the previous month's days and nights had been, but enough to wish she had a shawl. She walked down the broad steps that led to the garden. It wasn't a deep garden; however, the clever landscaping gave the illusion of more depth than there was. Paths wound around bushes, trees, and small flower beds. The three-quarters moon illuminated the area enough for walking. Her heart rate slowed as she meandered along the paths. She saw a large black cat stalking something, then stop to stare up at her as she approached. As it ran away, she smiled. She breathed in deeply, catching the hint of roses perfuming the air. It felt so peaceful out in the garden. So normal.

Her thoughts wandered as she strolled through the garden, but invariably wandered to Harry.

In his way, Harry had been a good man. As good as he could have been, she supposed, given his upbringing and career. She'd loved him as a dutiful wife; however, she'd never been *in love* with him. Now she understood that difference. The grief she felt after his death was more for what had not been in their marriage.

She stopped by a small fountain that rippled softly. She raised her face to the moonlight, closed her eyes and breathed in deeply.

~

IT SURPRISED Aidan to find Gwinnie returned so quickly to the ballroom.

"Gwinnie, how is Lady Blessingame?" he asked.

"She wasn't in Father's study."

Aidan stared at her. "She wasn't?"

"No. No one was there. The only sign someone had been in there was a crumpled man's handkerchief on one of the chairs by the fireplace."

"Have you seen her or her brother since you returned to the ballroom?"

She shook her head.

Aidan looked about, searching for the two. "Perhaps she returned to her room," he mused. He looked at Gwinnie. "Could you—"

She sighed. "Could I check on her? Yes, I can check on her," Gwinnie said with a wry smile.

"It's not what you think," he said gruffly, noting her expression.

"I'm sure," she said drily. She turned to walk toward the stair. "I'll be back shortly," she said over her shoulder.

"Thank you," Aidan replied absently, as his eyes roamed the ballroom again.

In his gut, he didn't think Bella had returned to her room. But where would she have gone? What was she doing?—And where was Melville?

He checked the refreshments alcove, then went

downstairs to check the formal dining room, as Melville might have been assigned the first sitting. Neither he nor Bella were to be found.

A GUNSHOT SHATTERED the peace of the garden.

Bella gasped as she looked wildly around. Where had it come from? The terrace, she thought.

Instinctively crouching slightly as Harry taught her at the sound of gunfire, she grabbed her skirts up and ran swiftly in the shot's direction, her heart pounding in her chest. The beautiful intricate garden layout, a pleasure to meander through, now became a hinderance. It ensured she must run away from the sound before she could run toward it.

She ran up the terrace steps and looked wildly about. Above her, people were leaning out the ballroom windows.

"Do you see anything?" she called out.

She heard a small chorus of *no's* and saw shaking heads.

"Wait!" she heard a young woman call out. "That way!" she yelled, pointing off to Bella's right, "at the end of the terrace."

Bella looked in that direction. It was dark there; no moonlight illuminated that end, as a large tree shaded the area. But she saw a darker shape near the corner. A man lay there. As she reached his side and squatted down beside him, she heard the terrace doors from the main hall slam open, rattling the wall of windows.

He breathed yet. When she touched him to see where he was shot, he turned his head in her direction, his breathing ragged. He'd been shot in his chest. She pressed her hands over his wound and pressed down, as the women of Brussels had taught her to do for the soldiers shot or stabbed following the battle at Quatre Bras when all nationalities of injured poured into the city.

"Lord Candelstone!" cried a choked male voice behind her.

She turned her head to look up. She did not recognize the young man who stood frozen beside her. Luckily, Aidan was the next person out the door. He pushed the man aside and crouched down beside her.

"He's been shot in the chest! We need to stop the bleeding!" she cried frantically, as blood seeped around her gloved fingers. He was bleeding heavily. Bella's heart constricted. She may despise the man and his machinations, but he did not deserve to die.

More people surged out the terrace doors to see what was going on. Servants shoved through them to bring linens and lanterns. Aidan grabbed a thick pad and put it under her blood-soaked gloved hand, where she pressed it down on the wound. It quickly turned bright red. Vaguely, Bella knew her dress carried bloodstains as well.

"Candelstone! Who shot you? Did you see them?" Aidan asked.

Candelstone's eyelids fluttered a moment and a small, indecipherable sound came from his lips, then he lost consciousness.

"Get Merlin!" Aidan shouted at the servants.

"I'm coming!" he heard from in the house, on the other side of the crowd.

"William!" shrieked Lady Candelstone, pushing her way through people. "William!"

Aidan quickly rose to his feet. He grabbed his elder sister, stopping her from throwing herself across her husband. "He's still alive. Lady Blessingame is pressing a pad tight against the wound."

Dr. Merlin Nowlton dropped to his knees on the other side of Candelstone. "Can you keep the pressure on the wound a few moments longer, Lady Blessingame?" he asked her.

"Yes," she replied, though her wrists and forearms had started to shake. She leaned in to press harder.

Dr. Nowlton yanked off his neckcloth. "Aidan, your neckcloth, please," he said as he loosened Candelstone's neckcloth to remove it as well. Aidan yanked his off and tossed it to his nephew. Dr. Nowlton tied them together. He jerked his head at the servant holding a lantern.

"Put the lantern down. We're going to need your help as well. Good. Now, in a moment, I am going to have Lady Blessingame remove her hands. Aidan, you will grab one end of the neckcloths, while I the other. You, Stephen," he said, addressing the servant, "will raise Lord Candelstone by his shoulders enough that Mr. Nowlton and I will pass the ends of the neckcloths around his back to bring it forward to bind it tightly in front over the pad. Does everyone understand?"

Aidan took his end of the tied neckcloths as they all said *yes*.

"Now, Lady Blessingame."

Swiftly, the men got the temporary bandage tied around Lord Candelstone's barrel chest.

Bella rose shakily to her feet. Her hands, through the evening gloves, were wet with Lord Candelstone's blood. Large blood drops dotted the front of her gown. She felt exhausted and suddenly light-headed. She swayed slightly.

Aidan saw her weakness and caught her before

she could faint. He guided her to a stone bench along the terrace wall.

"Sit," he said harshly. Then amended his tone, "I'll send someone to you. You were amazing."

"Thank you," she murmured.

She slowly stripped off the ruined gloves and dropped them to the ground beside her. She wished she had a cloth to wipe her hands on, though they seemed to dry quickly to a sticky consistency in the evening air. With a sigh, she leaned down to clear her head and wipe her hands on the only cloth available to her, the hem of her ruined gown.

When she sat up again and looked around, it appeared all the ball's guests were now on the terrace, milling about, chattering together. She saw Lady Malmsby making shooing motions to get their guests to return indoors. Ann and Ellinbourne crossed the terrace toward Bella.

"Bella!" Ann called out as they hurried toward her. "Bella! Are you okay?"

"Yes. I believe I just stood too fast and felt light-headed for a moment. I am quite recovered," she assured her friend. "But you should not be by me, you should see to your guests," Bella gently admonished.

"We had to make sure you were all right first," Ellinbourne said.

Ann nodded vigorously. "It was wonderful what you did. I don't think I could have."

Bella shook her head. "In some moments, it is amazing what we are called upon to do and can do." She took in a deep breath. "Though I'll own, I am now exhausted by the event. And shaky, too, if I am honest. A plentitude of nerves, I fear. I need to retire to my room."

"I'll request a hot bath be drawn for you," Ann said.

Bella smiled wanly. "That would be lovely. Thank you, but the servants are much too busy with the ball. If you could just send my maid with a pitcher of hot water—"

"Easily," Ann said.

Bella leaned over to pick up the bloody gloves to take them into the house. A dark shape drew her attention. She reached under the bench.

"What is it?" Ellinbourne asked.

Bella pulled out a small pistol. "A muff pistol," she said, as she studied the weapon lying along the palm of her hand. It was a small, elegant piece, with gold veining incised down the barrel and a companion floral motif inlaid over the butt of the pistol.

Ellinbourne frowned. He took the small gun from her and examined it.

"I had one when I was in Brussels," Bella told them, "But not as fancy as this one. Mine had scrimshaw on the handle," she said absently. She frowned, remembering those days.

"Did you ever use it?" Ann asked tentatively.

"Once," Bella replied honestly before she could stop herself. She didn't want to talk about that time and didn't want Ann or Ellinbourne to ask. "I don't think it has been under the bench long. I think that is the weapon used on Lord Candelstone. Though his wound bled a great deal, the wound was not large. Something a small caliber gun like this might cause."

Ellinbourne agreed.

Bella stood up. Another wave of dizziness assailed her. She grabbed on to the Duke's forearm to keep from falling.

"Are you sure you are well?" he asked, as he steadied her.

'I will be," she assured him, letting go of his arm. "I'm going to slip away up the servants' staircase. You return to your guests. I'm fine now, but I do thank you for your concern."

"What about the pistol?" Ann asked.

Bella glanced down at the gun the Duke held.

"I'll take it," Ellinbourne said. He stuck it in his jacket pocket. "And I'll see that Nowlton gets it. He is too preoccupied with Lord Candelstone to bring it to his attention at the moment."

"Thank you, your grace," Bella said. She skirted around Ann and walked swiftly to the side door she'd used earlier to get to the terrace and slowly climbed the stairs.

She laid the ruined gloves on her vanity. The events of the evening continued to affect her. She felt shaky and weak, quite like she had the evening she shot the Vizconde Miguel Carrasco-Torres.

CHAPTER 7

DR. MERLIN NOWLTON

Lady Malmsby, after consultation with Mr. Harold, suggested a drapery from the music room for a makeshift litter.

"It will get bloody, and you'll never get the blood out," Merlin warned.

"I know. It will afford me an excuse to replace them," she said blithely.

Lady Catherine suddenly sobbed loudly as the men organized the makeshift litter.

"Catherine!" chastised Lady Malmsby. "Enough drama. We don't have time for you to enact a Cheltenham tragedy. You need to assist Merlin. If you cannot provide the help he requires, you cannot be in the room while Merlin attends to Candelstone. You can't have it both ways, you can't indulge in dramatic histrionics and be a helper for the doctor. It is one or the other. You must decide and decide now."

Lady Catherine stopped crying, though her face looked like crumpled paper. She gave one more shuddering sniff.

She hovered behind and beside the men, continually wringing her hands. As they carried Candelstone upstairs in their makeshift litter, she clung to the balustrade with one hand while in the other she clenched a handkerchief tight against her mouth. At the top of the stairs, as they maneuvered him into the bedroom, she pulled it away and waved it to get attention. "Don't you think we should send for Dr. Walton?" she asked.

"Why, when we have an excellent doctor in the house?" asked Lady Malmsby, trailing behind her.

"But Merlin is so young," Lady Catherine said, wringing her hands again. "And he wears spectacles. Does he have the knowledge to treat my dear William?"

"Catherine! Have you paid no attention to the family? Merlin has had years of extensive medical education in Scotland!" declared Lady Malmsby.

Merlin laughed. "Don't fret, Grandmother. I often get doubts due to my age." He directed the men on how to get Lord Candelstone gently in the bed with the least pain for his lordship, then looked toward his aunt. "I assure you, Aunt Catherine, I have extensive training with some of the best surgeons in Edinburgh. It would take too long to call Dr. Walton to come here and Candelstone needs help *now*. Immediate care is often the difference between life and death."

Lady Catherine whimpered agreement, still wringing her hands.

Merlin looked up at Mr. Harold, who stood off to the side. "Please fetch my medical bag from my room. I should also like two bowls of hot water and more linens for cleansing and binding the wound."

Mr. Harold nodded and left the room. When he returned with Merlin's bag, two maids accompanied him with linens draped over their arms, each carrying a washbowl and a pitcher of hot water. They set about organizing the area for Merlin's surgery as if they had done it many times before.

Merlin nodded in appreciation. "Thank you." He turned again to Mr. Harold. "I'm sorry, could you also procure a bottle of wine and a glass?" he asked. He took a Tincture of Opium out of his bag and held it up to the light to check the volume. "I'd like one footman to stay and to help me shift Candelstone around as necessary to bandage him. Aunt Catherine can stay if she stands behind me to hand me what I need when I need it, not to hover over her husband."

"Everyone else out of here," Merlin declared. "That includes you, Uncle Aidan," he said, staring at him through the top half of his thick eyeglasses.

Aidan nodded. "I'll be right outside if you need me."

"I won't," Merlin said dismissively. He poured some wine into the glass, then squeezed a few drops of the tincture into the wine. He stirred the mixture.

"Can you lift him a little for me?" Merlin asked the footman. "Let's see if we can get this into him," he told the man. He spotted Aidan still in the room. "Out!" he barked.

Aidan left the room and closed the door softly behind him, impressed at his nephew's take-charge ability.

He dragged a straight-back wood chair from down the hallway to beside the door, then collapsed into the chair. Leaning forward, elbows on his knees, he laid his face in his hands as he closed his eyes and thought of the evening.

It had been a night for emotions. He held his close

in, though they clawed at his insides like caged beasts. He wanted to go out into the night and scream until he had no more breath left to scream with. But he couldn't, for that was not the man others depended on. That was not the steady, responsible gallery owner. The stalwart protector of the family, the one to keep everything together when the world goes mad.

God, some days he hated his family role. They were so carefree and boisterous, trusting him to set things straight. Tonight, he wanted someone to share the weight. Not take it away, but ease it.

He straightened and leaned his head back. He breathed in deeply once, twice, willing the beast back in its cage, those claws sheathed. Time for plans, not emotion.

The guests need to be interviewed. Did anyone see anything? He should contact Mr. Martin, the Bow Street Runner who had helped them last month at Versely Park. They would talk to him; he had that way about him. And Bella. Someone needed to talk to Bella. How had she been there? When he glanced back at her to assure himself she was all right, he saw her hand something to Ellinbourne. It looked suspiciously like a small gun. But by Ellinbourne's lack of reaction, he didn't think it implicated Bella in anything, but how did she come to have it? Did anyone else see her? He acknowledged he was watching her closely. He couldn't seem to keep his mind away from her. Was there truth in the tale she told him, or was that a web of lies as well?

Everything surrounding Candelstone seemed to be a tale within a tale, spun by a master spider. It did not surprise him that someone shot his brother-in-law. What he could find surprising is it had taken so many years for it to happen. But his nephew was an excellent doctor. If anyone could bring Candelstone through this, it would be Merlin. He was a magical being in medicine, as his namesake was with real magic.

There were soft footsteps in the hall. He opened his eyes. It was Gwinnie approaching.

"Grandmother sent me," she said.

"I don't know anything yet," he told her, rising to his feet. "Merlin is still in there with him. He ordered me out."

She shook her head. "I'm not here about Uncle. Grandmother wanted to know how *you* are doing. She said this has been a trying night for you."

He looked at her in surprise. "Yes," he affirmed, nodding. He compressed his lips. "Yes, it has been. I trust the worst is past us. What concerns me now is the stories society will create in whole cloth. They will decide who the guilty party is through guesswork, supposition, and things they thought they have seen or heard. You know that."

Gwinnie bit her lower lip. "Yes, I do, but we will get the truth sorted... You know, Uncle has many enemies," she said.

"And by the events of this evening, I would say I am high on his list."

"And Bella as well."

"Yes, Bella as well." He shook his head at the mess that lay before them. "Once we know Candelstone's status, I will send for Mr. Martin."

"Is he the Bow Street Runner who was at the house party last month?"

"Yes."

She nodded. "I wish I had been there."

Aidan laughed as he remembered the house party. "You would have enjoyed it. Why weren't you?"

She shrugged. "Previous commitments."

"You know, we may be here awhile, waiting. Sit down in this chair, I'll get another," he said.

They sat down next to each other to wait. It was quiet save for the faint strains of music coming from the ballroom upstairs. Gwinnie listened, swaying gently to the music. "How odd, there should be a ball still going on," she said. "I'm surprised people haven't left."

"It is curiosity that is keeping them here, not the enjoyment of a ball," Aidan said caustically.

"Poor Ellinbourne and Ann, to have their betrothal ball so ruined in this way," said Gwinnie.

Aidan shrugged. "The ball is more for the family than for Ann and Ellinbourne. Primarily Ellinbourne's side of the family. He has a cavalcade of relations here."

"Yes, they are a lively bunch, and so nice. Our families will get along quite well, except maybe for Ellinbourne's youngest sister, the widowed Marchioness of Darkford," Gwinnie said, thinking of the woman she met that night who wore dark gray to a ball.

"Yes," Aidan said, "but she is scarcely out of her widow's weeds."

"You know, there remain rumors as to her husband's death. They say he was into occult practices."

"I'm impressed with Ellinbourne's sense of responsibility for his family. I believe he will take care of his sister," Aidan reassured her.

Gwinnie sighed. "I agree. It is just so sad to see an almost haunted melancholy in her eyes. Before I came up here, Lake was doing his best to jolly her, not that Lake is the jolliest of fellows at formal functions," she said ruefully.

The door opened behind them. Merlin came out, his glasses off, as he cleaned their thick lenses. He put his glasses back on and looked from Aidan to Gwinnie.

"I take it Grandmother sent you?" Merlin said to Gwinnie.

"Of course."

Merlin drew in a deep breath before he spoke. "It was a small caliber pistol into his upper shoulder. The bullet broke this bone here," he said, pointing to the spot on his own chest.

"His collarbone."

"Yes. We call it the clavicle bone. It appears a bone fragment nicked an artery, which is why there was so much blood. Luckily for him, Lady Blessingame put pressure down in the right place to slow that bleeding."

"Is he awake? Can I speak with him?"

"Not right now. I gave him more of the Tincture of Opium, so he should sleep through the night."

"Did he see who shot at him?"

Merlin shook his head. "Aunt Catherine asked him that. Said he came outside to get some air and take a pinch of snuff. Heard someone call his name, turned, and was shot but he didn't see who did it."

"Male or female?"

Merlin shook his head again. "Aunt Catherine did not ask him that. People are still here?"

"Yes. Ghouls, like the characters in Lake's books," Aidan said.

"Shows you, Lake does not stray far from human nature in his gothic novels," Gwinnie said. "They are staying to hear what happens with Uncle. When I came downstairs, there wasn't much dancing, just some of the youngest guests. Everyone else is standing around gossiping and speculating."

"Then I should go upstairs and make an announcement as to Candelstone's condition," Aidan said.

"I'll go with you," Gwinnie said.

"Coming, Merlin?"

He shook his head. "I need to clean up."

Nowlton nodded and walked purposefully toward the stairway, Gwinnie behind him, hurrying to catch up.

"I'll tell the musicians to stop playing," she said breathlessly.

He nodded.

Gwinnie ran ahead, threading her way through the milling crowd of guests. Aidan stopped at the entrance. When people saw him, they stopped talking. Ellinbourne and Ann came up beside him, followed by the Dowager Duchess, the Duke, and Lord Lakehurst.

"He'll live," Aidan told them softly.

"We should make an announcement," the Dowager Duchess said, as the music ceased.

"I intend to," Aidan said.

Captain Melville pushed his way through the crowds. "Where is my sister?" he demanded. "I demand to see my sister."

"Your sister has gone to her room," Ann said, glaring at him. "She needed to change out of her bloodied clothes and to relax. She's been quite traumatized by what she did to help save Lord Candelstone. I sent up a sleeping draught for her."

"Oh. You haven't locked her away anywhere?"

"For what?"

"For shooting Lord Candelstone."

Some of the nearest guests gathered closer.

Aidan ground his teeth. "She didn't shoot Lord Candelstone. Why would you say that?"

"That's what some people are saying," Melville whined.

"They are wrong," Aidan forcefully said. He looked balefully around at the nearest guests, then back at Melville. "That's a ridiculous supposition. Come join us for breakfast tomorrow. You can see her then," he told him.

Pouting, Captain Melville left.

Ellinbourne grabbed Ann's hand as they stood beside Aidan. Gwinnie remained with the musicians.

"I should tell you," Ellinbourne said, leaning toward Nowlton, lowering his voice. "Lady Blessingame found a gun under the bench."

Nowlton's head whipped around to look at Ellinbourne.

"Muff pistol," he said. "I have it in my pocket."

Nowlton frowned and nodded, then turned back to face those in the ballroom. The room went quiet.

"Someone shot Lord Candelstone with a small caliber bullet. It hit his collarbone. The doctor has successfully operated on him, and my brother-in-law is now resting comfortably. Barring any infection, he should make a complete recovery. Lady Candelstone asked him if he saw who shot him. He replied *no*. That is all we can tell you at the moment. If anyone saw anything, we ask that you inform us. We will contact Bow Street to help with this investigation."

"I have already sent word requesting Mr. Martin's presence early tomorrow if he is in town," Lady Malmsby said.

Aidan looked at her in surprise for sending for the runner so quickly, but nodded. "Excellent," he said.

Ellinbourne stepped forward to address the guests, Ann close beside him. "Miss Hallowell and I thank you for coming to our betrothal ball. This is not how we wished our ball to end, but end it must for the sake of the Nowlton family," Ellinbourne said. "We are, however, grateful that you were present to hear Lord Candelstone's injury is not serious."

The guests' voices began again, the volume rising. Slowly, reluctantly, they made their way past the family, many stopping to offer best wishes to Lord Candelstone and offering what they saw. Some ventured to echo Captain Melville's fear; however, Nowlton's reaction shut them down quickly.

The family thanked them. It was an hour past midnight before the last guest left, to the accompaniment of Don Joaquín Pedroso y Castel softly playing his guitar.

~

WHILE ANN, Gwinnie, and Lady Malmsby went to check on Bella, Aidan, Ellinbourne, Malmsby, and Lake gathered in the Duke's old study on the same floor as the ballroom. They took seats at the round table in the center of the room. Mr. Harold brought them brandy. Malmsby raised his glass. "To the 1816 Knights of the Round Table!"

Everyone but Aidan laughed. He scowled.

"What are we going to do about Captain Melville?" Ellinbourne asked, as they all settled after the toast. "His voice was loud enough to carry across the ballroom."

"Send him to deepest Africa," Aidan said tiredly.

"With Candelstone," Lake suggested.

Aidan snorted. "Agreed."

"Before I forget," said Ellinbourne. He reached into a jacket pocket. "Here is the weapon Lady Blessingame found. We believe it is likely the weapon used, though I should like Merlin to look at it to confirm. It was too clean to have been under that bench long."

"You say you were with her when she found it?" the Duke asked.

"Yes. She had dropped her bloodied gloves on the ground after she stripped them off. When she decided to go to her room, she bent over to pick up the gloves and her fingers brushed against the gun. She pulled it out. Called it rightly a muff pistol and told Ann she had had one once, and she had used it as well. She said hers had a scrimshaw handle, not this unique gold etching."

"It is an expensive little toy," Lake observed, picking the gun up to examine it.

"Yes. So, who here, besides Lady Blessingame and me, would have motivation to shoot Candelstone?"

"You? why you?" Lake asked.

Aidan laughed harshly as he rose from the round table to pick up the packet of letters from where he and Bella had left them. He returned to the table and waved them.

"Because today I learned of Candelstone's role in turning Lady Blessingame and me from our courtship, and of his encouraging Sir Harry to marry her instead."

"I remember when you were courting her," Lake said. "Never heard what happened."

Aidan grunted. "It's here," he said, dropping the packet of letters on the table.

Malmsby drew them close to look at them.

"Candelstone and Sir Harry conspired. You probably are not aware that Lady Blessingame is a talented cryptographer. Candelstone wanted her to work for the War Office and felt I would not allow her to do so. He was most likely correct in that regard. He told Sir Harry to split us apart and encouraged Harry to marry her himself."

"How did he do that?"

"Harry convinced me that Bella was propositioning other men, that she was no longer a virgin, that she had even propositioned him. Idiot fool that I was, I believed him. I did not trust that the beautiful, charming creature I had would actually want to marry me. If I would have just talked to her, we would have cleared up the issue; however, Harry had been cleverer with the deception for Bella. He forged my signature in the betting books at White's with a bet I would bed her before the season was done. Made sure Captain Melville saw that bet, as well."

"Egad, learning this, Lady Blessingame felt betrayed and turned to Sir Harry for solace," summarized Malmsby, looking up from the letters.

"That is correct."

"How is it you did not find this out before now?" Ellinbourne asked.

"Lady Blessingame just received that packet of letters yesterday from Sir Harry's solicitor. Candelstone's orders, suggestions, and congratulations to Sir Harry are in these letters."

"Have you read these letters?" Ellinbourne asked.

"I skimmed them. I hope to read them closer tomorrow."

"You should," said his brother, who pushed the letters back toward him. He shook his head. "Lord Candelstone's arrogance is amazing, and we have known the man for what, almost our entire lives?" he reflected.

"Lady Blessingame also told me Candelstone has been in contact with her, demanding she come back to work for him."

"But isn't he retired?" Lake asked.

"Officially from the government, yes. But he is now part of a private group that is afraid of terrorists in our country, like those that caused Penderson mill to burn down."

"The events at the Duchess's house party did not squelch his desire to recruit?" asked Ellinbourne.

"No," Aidan said, disgusted. "I wish Mother had sent them to the other side of the world, as she has so often threatened."

"She wouldn't do that, not really," Lake said. "Catherine is her favorite, even if she did marry Lord Candelstone."

"Unfortunately, I agree with you," Aidan said.

"I'll see what I can do," Malmsby said. "I have an idea."

Aidan rose from his chair. "I'm for bed. Mr. Martin will be here early in the morning asking lots of questions. I'll need a good sleep to keep up with him."

"I'm looking forward to meeting this Mr. Martin," Lake said.

"A very smart man, obviously more educated than his kind, but closed mouth on that. Has a kind soul, too. He has a child from the streets that he has taken on as his protégé.

"How did you come to know him?" Arthur asked.

"Sir James and Lady Branstoke recommended him. They've worked with him. If they had been here tonight, they would have leaped into the investigation, but they are at their estate in Kent as Lady Branstoke is increasing," Aidan told them.

"Goodnight, gentlemen," he said, to an echo of *goodnights* from Malmsby's modern Knights of the Round Table.

CHAPTER 8

BOW STREET

M r. Harold showed Mr. Martin into the Malmsby House breakfast parlor at half-past eight. Aidan rose as he entered.

He reached out his hand to Mr. Martin. "Good to see you again. But where is Daniel?" Aidan asked, referring to the young mudlark Mr. Martin had taken on as a protege.

"The Earl of Soothcoor took him and some other charity boys to Northumberland for the summer."

"Northumberland! Being London city boys, I wonder how they will make out—or how Soothcoor will make out," Aidan said, laughing, trying to imagine the dour Earl of Soothcoor with a handful of young boys. That painting wouldn't come to life in his mind's eye.

"He felt he owed them, as they helped rescue his young nephew last December," Mr. Martin explained.

Aidan nodded. "Well, we are happy you are here. Please sit. Jimmy," he said to the young footman who stood to the side of the room, "please get a plate for Mr. Martin." He resumed his seat as Mr. Martin sat as well. "I don't know what the Duchess told you in her note—"

"Just that there had been an incident at Ellinbourne's and Miss Hallowell's betrothal ball last night that could use my help in resolving."

Aidan snorted. "An *incident*! That is an understatement. Parties unknown shot Lord Candelstone."

"Lord Candelstone shot? I saw nothing in the papers about that this morning," Mr. Martin said.

"It wouldn't have made the papers as they did not kill him. They shot him with a small caliber gun last night on the back terrace. Lady Blessingame later found the weapon under a bench on the terrace."

Mr. Martin put down his coffee and drew a notebook and a pencil stub out of his pocket. "What time did this occur, and where?"

"Fairly early in the ball. The musicians had just taken a slight break and the first seating for supper had been announced. About eleven, I'd say. Candelstone was on the terrace."

"Was he alone?"

"I don't know. However, Lady Blessingame had been walking in the garden when she heard the shot and rushed up to the terrace. She found Lord Candelstone and immediately put pressure on the wound to staunch the blood until help could arrive. I think I was first or second there."

He thought a moment. "Second, there was a young man there before me. I had to push him out of my way. But others quickly followed. People were pouring out on to the terrace or leaning out the ballroom windows to see what was going on."

"And you say she was the one to find the gun?"

"She had nothing to do with the shooting," Aidan peremptorily said.

Mr. Martin raised an eyebrow at him. "And how is it you know that?" he asked levelly. "Were you in the garden with the lady?"

"No."

Mr. Martin silently regarded him.

"I admit, the lady had good reason to want to shoot him, if she was of that nature—as did I last night, as well." He compressed his lips together. Then sighed out deeply. "She had recently discovered—and told me—she had proof Lord Candelstone had been responsible for our courtship faltering three years ago."

This time, both of Mr. Martin's eyebrows pulled upward.

"Sir Harry Blessingame worked for Lord Candelstone. Candelstone ordered Harry to take what course of actions might be necessary to cause Lady Blessingame and me to end our relationship. Harry, for his part, came up with just the right artful lies to pull us apart. He knew us well. Lady Blessingame has the letters Candelstone wrote to Harry," Aidan finished bitterly.

"Hmmph," was the only sound Mr. Martin made at the end of Aidan's recital. He stared at him a moment, then looked down at his notebook to take more notes.

"How many people know this history you have related?"

"Just family—and Lady Blessingame's brother, Captain Melville."

"Any servants?"

Aidan blinked as he looked at Mr. Martin. "I don't know," he said slowly. "You are right to ask that question. We scarcely notice servants as they go about their work."

Mr. Martin nodded.

Aidan picked up his empty coffee cup and held it

up. The footman came forward to fill his cup and Mr. Martin's.

"Beg pardon, Mr. Nowlton. The staff knows," Jimmy reluctantly admitted.

Aidan started. "How?" he demanded.

Jimmy nervously rubbed the back of his neck. "Lady Blessingame had tea in the Duke's old study yesterday afternoon. When the maid went to pick up the tea tray and neaten the room afterward, she picked up the papers, think'n they be rubbish. Took 'em downstairs with the tea tray. One of the scullery maids read 'em as she likes ta read anythin'. Not many scullery maids ken read, ya' know, and it be a point o' pride, so she read 'em aloud..." His voice trailed off as Aidan put his head in his hands and groaned.

Mr. Martin chuckled.

"But they were back in the library last night," Aidan stated.

"Yes, Mr. Nowlton. Mr. Harold were right angry and told the maid to put them back where she found them."

"So, to your previous question, we add the servants to the list," Aidan reluctantly admitted, as his eyes followed Jimmy back to his post next to the breakfast buffet.

Mr. Martin gave him a crooked smile. "So, we will start here. You," he said, lifting his hand toward the footman. "What's your name?"

"Jimmy, sir."

"Did you hear the gunshot last night?"

"Yes sir, I—"

Aidan did not listen to Mr. Martin question Jimmy. In his mind, he went over the events at the ball, thinking of who was around and where they were. Who among them—beside himself and Lady

Blessingame—bore Lord Candelstone antipathy? It could be as few as one to a dozen. While he loved his slightly erratic sister, Catherine, he did not care for her husband. He didn't think anyone in the family did, only accepting him to family gatherings for the love they bore for Catherine. He knew he wouldn't be able to do that in the future.

~

BELLA WOKE DISORIENTED.

Her sleep had been rife with wild dreams.

She remembered dreaming of firing a pistol at Vizconde Miguel Carrasco-Torres, who'd been angry at her refusal of sexual favors.

He approached her with a bejeweled knife in his hand, a knife that glinted, mesmerizing, in the candlelight. He said he would use the knife to carve his initials on to her beautiful milk white breasts.

Terrified, she stepped backward, but stopped, realizing she stood on the edge of a cliff, where down below a turbulent sea crashed against jagged rocks. There was nowhere to go. She pulled the trigger of a pistol that had suddenly appeared in her hand. In that moment, the Vizconde changed into Lord Candelstone standing on the Malmsby House terrace. It was he who fell down in a widening pool of blood, a flow of blood she couldn't stem while the Vizconde stood on the other side of the terrace, laughing.

The blood changed from a spurt to a fountain and then to rain. Everything became drenched in blood, save for the Vizconde, standing in a circle of light where he played wild flamenco music on his guitar.

Bella sat up, shivering, as the last details of her dream drifted away, so real and unreal. She realized her breaths came short and fast, still caught in the dream's terror. She forced herself to relax. She closed her eyes and concentrated on relaxing one part of her body after another until the tightness was gone from her chest, and the horror of the nightmare receded.

Lord Candelstone.

She had to see how he was. Quickly, she splashed water left from the previous night on her face and cast off her night rail. She pulled a dark gray gown out of the wardrobe and put it on. She found soft black slippers on the bottom shelf of the wardrobe and slipped into those before turning to the vanity. She pulled her brush savagely through her hair, then wound the thick, dark hair into a bun at the top of her head and secured it with pins lying scattered on the vanity. She grabbed a handkerchief from the dresser in the corner and left her room.

The hall outside was quiet. She stood for a moment in the stillness. She realized she didn't know what room Lord Candelstone might be in. She walked slowly toward the stairs, listening as she went.

Down the hall, a door opened, and a servant came out of a room carrying a stacked breakfast tray.

"And bring coffee!" she heard from in the room. "None of that weak tea nonsense, no matter what Merlin says.—Ouch! Stop fussing, Catherine. Leave me alone!"

She'd found Candelstone.

She waited until the maid opened the door to the servant staircase, then she knocked on Candelstone's door.

Lady Catherine opened the door. She still wore her night wear and her mobcap over her papered hair. The skin under her eyes sagged. Bella wondered how much sleep the woman had been able to get during the night.

"Lady Blessingame," Lady Candelstone said, a rising note of surprise in her voice.

"I came to see how he is this morning. Since I could hear him bellow to the maid as she left, I suppose that is a sign he is much better," she said wryly, trying to get Lady Candelstone to smile as well.

A small smile graced the woman's lips. "We had a bit of a rough night, but he is better now."

"May I see him?"

Lady Candelstone turned toward the interior of the room. "Would you care for a visit from Lady Blessingame?"

"Yes. Let her in," he said gruffly.

She followed Lady Candelstone into the room, looking around as she did so. Their accommodations were a suite of rooms, not merely a bedroom, as she had. Judging by the soft feminine colors, the rooms had been Lady Candelstone's rooms growing up. A quilt jumbled on the settee by the window suggested Lady Candelstone's resting spot during the night. And not a comfortable one either. She touched the woman's arm.

"I'll sit with him if you would like to freshen up and get dressed," she told her.

Lady Candelstone looked at her husband, and then back at her. "I thank you. I think I shall." She crossed to the door to the dressing room. "I won't be long," she said, as she hesitated.

"I'll be here however long," Bella gently assured her.

Lady Candelstone nodded and closed the door behind her.

"So, what happened last night?" she briskly asked Candelstone as she crossed to the settee. She picked up the quilt to fold it up.

"I don't know."

"What do you mean, you don't know?"

"I don't know," he repeated emphatically. "I was in the ground-floor hall when I saw you out on the terrace. You went down the steps into the garden. I followed you outside."

"But you didn't come into the garden," Bella clarified. Inside she simmered, and she hadn't been in his presence five minutes. How could she get rid of this man—short of killing him? She must let emotions go. If they were to discover the shooter, she couldn't afford to succumb to her emotions. She'd already done that too much over the past few days.

"No, I thought to wait for you to return. I didn't know if you were taking the air or were meeting someone." He wiggled his eyebrows as he leered at her.

"You wanted to see what played out," she said levelly.

"He hesitated a moment, then, "Yes."

She nodded. "If I had seen you do that, I probably would have done the same," she admitted.

He smirked. "Yes. We are of a kind, you and I."

Her tight hold on her emotions exploded. "No! We are not. I will not be, I assure you," she angrily declared. She was not like Candelstone and would never be like Candelstone.

She threw the folded quilt over the back of the settee and sat down, pulling herself together, simmering in irritation.

He smiled and shrugged back at her, infuriating Bella more.

"What then?" she asked, the words dragged from her.

A knock on the bedroom door stopped him from

answering. Bella rose from the settee and crossed to open the door.

It was Aidan Nowlton and a man she didn't know. A man in a red vest.

A Bow Street Runner.

"Gentlemen," she said, as she stepped back and pulled the door open wider. "Please come in. Lord Candelstone was just telling me of the events last evening.

"Yes, we should like to hear those as well. Candelstone, you remember Mr. Martin from Versely Park last month, do you not?"

"The presumptuous footman. Yes, I do," he said sourly.

Mr. Martin smiled at Lord Candelstone.

"Lady Blessingame, I'd like you to meet Mr. Lewis Martin from Bow Street."

"Mr. Martin," she said, tipping her head ever so slightly. She wasn't certain if she would like him or not. He appeared too friendly to her suspicious mind.

"So, what happened last night?" Nowlton asked as he and Mr. Martin approached the bed.

"As I told Lady Blessingame, I saw her on the terrace and followed her out, but stayed on the terrace when she walked down into the garden."

"You did not follow her into the garden?" Mr. Martin asked for clarification.

"No, I did not wish to embarrass the lady if she perhaps had an assignation," he said archly.

Bella scowled at him. He would have her be the woman Harry led Nowlton to believe existed three years ago.

"Had you any reason to believe she would?"

"Well, no," Candelstone admitted. "But I wished to

talk to her. I went over to the side of the terrace as it was more shadowed over there."

"So you could ambush her," Nowlton said.

"What? No. Just to be out of the way of others," he declared. "But from behind me I heard a man say softly, *Not who I had wanted, but you'll do.* I whipped around then, right before he fired, regrettably not soon enough to see the miscreant," he said, scowling at his failure.

"You are certain it was a man?" Mr. Martin asked.

"Yes. I hit my head when I fell, stunned for a moment. Next thing I remember is Lady Blessingame pressing down on my chest. Hurt like hell, then I remember nothing until I was in this bed and Merlin stood over me, looking owl-eyed as he stared down at me through those ugly thick glasses of his."

"And this person, this man, said: *Not who I had wanted, but you'll do.* That phrase exactly, correct?"

Candelstone screwed up his expression as he thought. "No-o-o," he said slowly. "He said, *Not who I want, but you will do,*" he said.

Mr. Martin nodded and made a note on his pad.

"Is that significant?" Nowlton asked.

"Could be. Could show the man's a foreigner," he said as he made notes. He looked up. "For one, the shortened first part of the phrase is more active, speaking of now, and the second part without a contraction an English native might use, *you'll* versus *you will*. These are not definitive, but imply a possibility," Mr. Martin explained.

"Was there any hint of an accent?" Bella asked from her seat on the settee.

"The voice was too soft and raspy to determine."

"After my experiences working with you, I can certainly imagine you as the intended victim, but not as a second choice. Who would be the first choice?" Bella asked.

Mr. Martin and Mr. Nowlton nodded at her question.

"Yourself?" suggested Candelstone.

"Me! Why me?" she asked.

"Revenge for the Spanish Envoy?"

She looked at him, horrified. "No one knows about that!"

"I do, and if I do, others can."

"What's this about a Spanish Envoy?" Mr. Martin asked.

Candelstone laughed. "She killed him."

"Lord Candelstone!" yelled Bella. She surged to her feet. "How do you know that? Yes, I shot him; however, I don't know if he died," she said.

The door to the dressing room opened.

"I shot him with a similar gun to the one that shot you," Bella continued. "I might have killed him. I've been afraid that I've killed him, but I don't know that for a certainty, and that has haunted me for a year."

"You did everyone a favor," Candelstone said dismissively. "The man deserved to die. You know he killed Sir Harry, don't know?"

"Yes," she said in a quiet voice. "And the other two men with them as well. He told me in Brussels when he tied me up."

"See. He deserved to die," declared Candelstone. He clasped his hands together on top of the counterpane.

"If you knew all this, why did you send me to Brussels to spy on him?" Bella asked.

Candelstone shook his head. "I didn't send you there just to spy on him. Your cryptography skills were needed there. Having you available to monitor the Vizconde was a plus."

"You knew he would play with me because of Harry, didn't you? That he would eventually want to conquer me. Did you not care that those actions could put me in danger?"

He snorted. "Nonsense. I knew Harry trained you."

Bella's eyes widened. "And Harry died!" she yelled.

"It was a risk, yes, but if all went well, I achieved two objectives. Decipher French communications and neutralize Carrasco-Torres. I considered that a potential double win.

"But what about me? You have no feeling for anyone, do you? No sensibility as to the feelings of others, or that you might put them at risk."

"I had a plan."

"You, my lord, are a monster!" Bella declared.

She ran out of the bedroom, slamming the door behind her.

Aidan Nowlton went after her. Mr. Martin grabbed his arm and shook his head *no*.

"She will need time alone," Mr. Martin said. "There are more questions for Lord Candelstone. We need to figure out who the intended person might be, as they still may be a target. And we need to go over the guest list. Lord Candelstone, I'd like you to go over the guest list as well, to see if you see any names that might have a grievance with you or anyone else."

"I can get the list from the Duchess's secretary," Aidan said. "Most likely he has the correct list, including regrets and notes on who did not show, but who responded," Aidan said.

Mr. Martin nodded. "That will be good." He

looked up at Lord Candelstone. "So why were you following Lady Blessingame?"

"I wanted to talk to her."

"About what?" Mr. Martin asked, his pencil poised over his notebook again.

"I want her to work for me."

"Why?" Aidan demanded. "The war is over."

"On other shores, yes, but we have a rising risk within our own country, gentlemen, from dissidents, those who would do violence to achieve their ends. Our great country has become a leader in new inventions, inventions others are afraid of, so they lash out to stop it and all who support it. They don't want the world, or their corner of it, to change. They foment rebellion. And gentlemen, consider—we don't want anything like the French revolution on English soil."

"So, what is your intention?" Aidan asked. "You retired from government service last year."

"I, with some like-minded peers, am creating a private organization to investigate and root out these rebels."

"You are taking the King's law, and the responsibilities of the magistrates and barristers, and the courts of assize, into your own hands," Mr. Martin said.

"They cannot operate with the speed and agility we can!" he explained, growing excited, his eyes shining with the light of a fanatic, little different from those he would expose and destroy.

"I see," said Aidan levelly. "Do not count Lady Blessingame as part of your coterie. It should be clear to you she wants nothing more to do with spying."

Candelstone waved his hand dismissively. "Missish nonsense. She'll come around."

"Leave her alone."

"Or what?" Candelstone asked, bored with the conversation.

"Or Lady Malmsby will have her way."

Candelstone laugh crudely. "Faugh. For years, she has been threatening me with that. She loves Catherine too much. She was always her favorite, you know."

"William!" protested his wife. She scurried over to the side of the bed. "You shouldn't say such things!"

Candelstone turned to look at his wife. "Don't worry, my pet," he gently assured her. "She'll never do it, and at her age, I don't believe she has the connections to do so, either."

He looked back at Aidan and sneered. "Now go away, Mr. Gallery Owner, you and your posturing robin red-breast. My people will take care of this matter."

"You are a fool, Candelstone," Aidan said.

Candelstone laughed and shooed them away.

Aidan and Mr. Martin exchanged glances and left the room.

"He is certainly a man of many parts," Mr. Martin said quietly, as the door closed behind them. "What are you going to do?"

"I'm not certain. My concern right now is to learn who was the intended victim, family, or guest."

"What about Lady Blessingame?"

"What about her?" Aidan asked crossly. He didn't want to think about her yet—to do so would force him to face his shame in believing Harry's lies.

Mr. Martin grabbed his arm, stopping him. "Courage," he said. Then he dropped his hand and continued down the hall.

Aidan stood for a moment, then he joined Mr. Martin as he walked down the main staircase.

He saw Mr. Harold, the butler, come from the servants' wing. "Mr. Harold, do you know where the Duchess and Lady Blessingame might be found?"

"Her grace is meeting with the housekeeper. I have not seen Lady Blessingame."

"I saw her go into the Lady Margaret Parlor," offered the footman by the door.

"I'll take you to the Duchess's secretary for a copy of that guest list," Aidan told Mr. Martin. He looked down the hall. "Then I shall see about mustering that courage you spoke of."

CHAPTER 9
WHERE PAST AND PRESENT MEET

B ella sat in the Lady Margaret Parlor with its surfeit of pink decor, staring absently out the terrace door and windows that looked out on the terrace. In front of her was the stone bench she'd sat on the night before, and where she'd found the gun. No blood stains remained on the flagstone surface of the terrace. The servants had cleansed the area of blood and blood stains early in the morning.

The tears she'd cried while running from Lord Candelstone's room and down the stairs had dried on her cheeks. Her heart rate had resumed its steady beat. She sighed, her mind and memory back in Brussels in the days of Quatre Bras and Waterloo.

News of the tides of war changed hourly, as differing reports from the battlefields streamed in. She was with a group of diplomats of varying nationalities when the most cogent and believable report after Quatre Bras implied the French were winning. This belief lasted four hours or more. During this time, it became clear where true loyalties lay. Brussels women made French tri-color cockades and hung French flags from their homes. Some of the English who'd come to Brussels in Wellington's tail rushed to sell, for as little as a tenth of their original cost, belongings they'd purchased a month prior for hundreds of pounds.

The injured of all nationalities streamed into the city. Homes, churches, shops opened to tend to the injured who, when questioned, could not give them a true idea of the war. Regardless, the Brussels residents cared for all. Bella had joined the women of Brussels in tending to the injured. It was from them she learned about tourniquets and wound compression as they worked to save as many soldiers as they could.

It was while working with these women that Vizconde Miguel Carrasco-Torres, the Spanish envoy, found her.

In society, in the days leading up to the battle, he'd proclaimed himself a British ally. Now he crowed with delight at what he foresaw as the impending French victory. But he was a superstitious man, always making the sign of the cross on himself when he spoke of a French victory.

As he considered it bad luck to be near the injured, Bella let him pull her away from her nursing so as not to upset the others working around her, or the injured soldiers with their own worries. He took her to his hotel and told her if she became his mistress, he promised to protect her. If not, he would proclaim, to the victorious French, she was a British intelligence agent.

Bella refused. She taunted him with the seesaw nature of the reports from the battlefront. He assured her Napoleon would persevere, as he was a brilliant man, probably the most brilliant man in the world that day. He would ultimately be the ruler of Europe, and England, too, he told her.

Bella saw the wild light in his eyes. They glistened with vitality and fanatic belief.

"Two years ago, I knew one day you would be mine!" he said, as he tied her hands behind her back around a bedpost.

Bella stopped struggling to stare at him. "What do you mean?"

He laughed, then shook his head pityingly. "You have no clue how Sir Harry died, do you?"

"They ambushed him. You were there, you brought his body back."

"I killed him and our escort, then claimed an ambush. Gave myself a flesh wound to validate my participation. I was so bereft at the loss of my friend Sir Harry." He shook his head soulfully.

"Now, see how kind a man I am to beautiful ladies?" he'd said. "I have not made your bindings tight. The rope is long enough you can lie on the end of the bed to await my return," he told her, grinning.

Then he'd left her.

She'd tested her bindings. The knots were tight, but the length of rope between her hands was generous. She stood on the bed, then balanced on the footboard. She pulled her hands up behind her as far as she could. Her shoulders had screamed with pain. With her back pressed against the bed-post, she'd pushed herself up on her toes, but it wasn't enough. She sobbed in frustration. She tried again, this time bringing her hands together closer to the bedpost.

She worked on throwing the loose length of rope over the post. She didn't remember how many times she'd tried before she'd been successful. She lost her balance and fell forward on the floor. After that, it was easy to get her arms in front of her and worry the knots loose with her teeth. It was well dark before she was free.

What amazed her was the Vizconde hadn't searched her for weapons. From an inner petticoat pocket, she pulled out a gun and the small box of powder, ball, and tinder. She loaded her gun, her hands shaking, her shoulders aching.

There were steps outside the room. She ducked to the

other side of the room, from where a moment's opportunity might let her run to escape.

When the door opened, Bella pointed her gun and fired, just as Harry had taught her.

She leaped over the man lying in the doorway and ran out the door and down the hall. She ran outside. People were everywhere. Wellington won, they were proclaiming!

She stumbled twice but kept running toward the canals and their docks. She begged for passage to Antwerp, for she knew from there she could get back to England.

And she had.

Could the assailant's bullet that struck Lord Candelstone have been meant for her? And if actual harm was intended, why that small of a gun? Granted, a heart shot with a small caliber gun would have had the result of a larger caliber gun, but small guns with their short bores were notoriously finicky to aim.

How did Candelstone know she'd killed Carrasco-Torres? She laughed to herself. How could she ask that? Candelstone seemed to know everything. She wondered how long he'd known that the Vizconde had killed Harry? Interesting to consider, and in line with his crazy way of thinking, that he should ask her to get close to him.

She walked over to the door that led to the terrace. She reached for the door handle, but stopped. This door led directly to where Candelstone had been shot. She did not think she wanted to risk those memories flooding back to her, as her Brussels memories just had. She turned her back to the door and looked about the pink lady's room. The pink should have felt overwhelming, but somehow it didn't. She smiled.

Now that Aidan knew she had killed a man, she wondered what he thought of her? Would he hate her again? This time for a proper reason, not some artful lie?

She had missed him in the past three years. Once the hurt and anger and betrayal had slipped away, she found her old yearnings returning.

She saw he had changed over the last three years. She recognized he wasn't the man she fell in love with. Honestly, she thought she liked, maybe even loved, this man better. There was a groundedness within him, a firm center. He reminded her of Atlas holding the world on his shoulders. But despite all that, he cared for his family, for what happened to them, for taking care of them in a way that touched her heart.

She knew that was the type of man her brother wanted to be and failed. Her poor brother was not a wicked man, though he certainly lacked the wisdom and maturity Aidan possessed. Harry certainly had Aidan's intelligence, but he'd lacked his steadiness and his wisdom. Aidan was the Duke in all but the title. Not that she didn't like the current Duke or the Duke's heir, but Aidan took on so much for them.

She wondered if they—or anyone—were aware. Sadly, her love for Aidan hadn't died three years ago. It burned on.

But it was too late.

～

AFTER INTRODUCING Mr. Martin to the secretary, Aidan walked slowly back to the ground floor main hall. He stared at his boot toes as he walked, almost running into a maid carrying fresh linens, his mind churning. He looked up then and took a deep breath.

Mr. Martin was correct. He was afraid. And embarrassed. And shamed. A host of emotions ran through his head and heart, creating chaos down to his very soul. He was a fool. Now as well as three years ago.

Bloody Hell! How could he have been such a fool?

Easily.

Harry had played upon the bonds of brotherhood formed in school and on into university years.

He'd brought Harry into the family, introduced him to everyone. He made friends easily and by making friends with everyone around him, he'd lifted some of the shy reticence from Aidan. Following Harry's example, Aidan learned how to be more at ease with people. If it hadn't been for observing Harry's ways, Aidan didn't think he would have had the courage to approach Miss Melville almost four years ago. Though in his late twenties, back then, he'd still had a bit of the bumbling schoolboy in him. Now he was just a humorless merchant.

He felt they owed Lady Blessingame happiness. She was the one who had suffered the most through meeting his family. What could he do? What could the family do to make up for all she'd lost? Her life took a turn far different from what she would have imagined, that any young debutante would have imagined. She should have enjoyed her London Season and not been pulled into a web of lies.

Candelstone believed he could get her to work for him again. His family needed to show her their support, so she didn't feel she had no options.

They couldn't change the past, but they could help her make a better future. He would task his mother with matchmaking for her.

He tapped lightly on the closed Lady Margaret Parlor door and heard a faint, "Come in."

Lady Blessingame stood near the door that led out to the terrace.

She glanced at who came in, then turned back to the door.

"The Duke is to be commended," she said. "This door is in perfect working order. Not a squeak or a click." She opened the terrace door silently, then closed it again with only a whisper of sound. "At a ball with people all around, laughing, talking, walking, one wouldn't hear that ever-so-slight *snick* when the door closed. And there is no squeak at all. If I remember correctly, the door leading from the main hall to the terrace has a slight squeak."

Aidan walked across the room to stand beside her. Her eyes were bright, but red-rimmed, her color high, but the worst from her bout of tears had faded.

It was obvious she did not want to discuss any of what went on in Lord Candelstone's room. He would cooperate, for now.

"You think this is the door used by the person who shot Lord Candelstone?"

"I do. This room was not lit. I remember Lady Malmsby saying something about wanting to dissuade guests from coming into this room." She laughed slightly. "She said there were plenty of other rooms available for assignations."

"This has long been Mother's favorite room, which one could consider odd, as the decor is not at all in her style."

Bella looked back at the room. "Yes, she is not a fussy woman, yet this room is the epitome of fussy."

"But from a composition standpoint, it works well," Aidan said. "I'm actually surprised a painting has never been done of this room."

Bella nodded, then looked back out the door. "But someone used the room last night. There are bits of nature on the floor here."

Aidan looked down. There were a few pieces of leaves and dirt by the doorsill. "As no one was to be in here, the maids would have no reason to clean here today."

"Such was my thought," Bella said. "I don't believe someone was waiting here long for their victim, or a victim, as it might be. If they had been, their aim would have been truer, as it is near to here where Candelstone fell. And if they tossed the gun afterward, in an underhanded toss, it could easily have skidded into that shadowed corner under the bench where I found it."

"I see that," Aidan agreed.

She tilted her head as she studied the outside. "The shooting was a spontaneous, and dangerous, last-moment decision by the shooter, which is why the gun was tossed away."

By unspoken agreement they walked out of the parlor into the hall.

"How many doors are there to the terrace?" she asked a moment later.

"Five. One at the end of each wing that are narrow, and more for servant use, and three along the main length of the terrace—the door here, the one in the hall, and one from the music room across the hall. Why do you ask?"

She shrugged. "Trying to visualize everything. I came out the servants' door on the far right," she said, pointing to the door, "and walked across the terrace to the steps down to the garden. There was no one about, but the musicians hadn't started another piece. I knew if they had gone on break, people would come out here to get fresh air. I wanted to get into the garden first and find a spot where I could be alone. Gwinnie gave me a tour the other day, and I remembered benches. I wanted to find one."

"It is an ideal garden for contemplation," Aidan said. "Might you walk in the garden with me now?"

She looked up at him, suspicious. "Why?"

"For contemplation."

Bella laughed shortly. "I don't know if I am ready for that."

"That is understandable. My mind is in a turmoil, as I know yours has been. What if I promise not to talk about us, about what was or might have been?" Aidan said.

"Then why do you wish to talk to me?" she asked, wary.

"To learn about the world you, Lord Candelstone, and Harry inhabited. To try to understand the—I don't know—the loyalty, I guess, that they clung to so tightly that it warped who they were. To make sense of my turmoil from another angle."

"I don't know what I can tell you," she said. "But I can understand your curiosity. Yes, let's walk and talk," she said, walking toward the terrace door.

"Won't you need a bonnet?" he asked. His mother and sisters would never have gone out into the sun without one.

"I should.—La, life is full of *shoulds* for us, isn't it? I'll toss my shawl over my head and pull it forward to shade my face," she said, pulling her shawl on top of her head and pulling it forward.

Aidan opened the door and led her outside. He offered her his arm. She looked at him for a moment. Then smiled and accepted the courtesy, slipping her hand in his arm. With her other hand, she held the sides of her shawl together so it wouldn't blow off her head.

"You do that a great deal, don't you?" Bella said as they cross the terrace to the steps.

"Do what?"

"Watch out for the care of others."

He shook his head. "I don't know what you mean."

"Just now, you voiced concern for my going out without a bonnet. You were correct; however, I don't know of many men who would have done so."

He frowned. "I don't know. I believe a man should look out for others, especially women and children. It is our duty, our role."

"Why?"

His frowned deepened. "It is what men have been taught for hundreds of years."

"Not all men. Take, for example, Harry and Lord Candelstone. They, too, believe it is their responsibility to look out for others; however, in their circumstances, the *other* is their country, their leaders. They know of no other way of being. Those things you do naturally for your family, for women, children, and others, are what they do naturally for their country."

"I don't know the forces which propelled Lord Candelstone to this belief," she continued, "but you knew Harry for years. You can understand what pushed Harry that way. His family! They did not care about him, at least not in the way he wished them to. There were too many of them and no opportune time to spend more time with one child over another. Plus their standard of living, spread out over all of them, was to always appear to be middle-class gentry. He didn't believe they had loyalty, or even love for each other. I think they did. How else could they have struggled so hard to see to his education? Harry didn't see that. What Harry saw was that, if you had love for the country, you expected nothing in return, but when they rewarded you for what you did—ah, bliss."

Aidan's brow furrowed. "But a country is only a construct of ideas, laws, and agreements."

"Yes, and a country cannot not fill a person's emotional well. A person could convince themselves that they didn't suffer a loss for not getting that love and care in return. That was not what *country* was capable of doing in return. But in their mind, the country gave them what they missed in childhood. Recognition. There was prize money and the possibility of rising in rank. Harry felt great pride for his knighthood, you know. With his knighthood, he was higher than his family, who he felt didn't pay attention to him as a child."

"You," she went on, "always knew your family loved you, and you loved them. When they ask for your help, you are happy to do so, and they always thanked you and showed their appreciation." She turned her head to look at him, her head cocked. "But I would wager they now take your actions for granted, and so do you."

"What do you mean?" he asked, frowning again.

"You don't get thanks for what you do, they—and you—take your actions for granted. The family considers you more duke than your brother or his son, and they are happy to let you do so. They all agree you are steadier than anyone else and better able to handle things." She shook her head. "I disagree. I think it is cunningness on their part."

"Cunningness!"

"Yes. I see your brother at meals and other odd times. He is a highly intelligent man. He is not the absent-minded academic the family joke him to be."

"Oh, you don't know Lord Malmsby. He is absent-minded."

"If something does not interest him, he will not do it. He'll wait and see if someone else will pick up that task. He has excellent stewards in place on his estates, true?"

"Yes, he has some of the best managed properties in the entire country."

"Who hired them?"

"He did, in consultation with his solicitors."

"And you assumed it was more solicitors than Lord Malmsby, didn't you?" Bella smiled. "You should talk to those solicitors. Does he ignore his parliamentary commitments?"

"No. He votes, but he is not active in debates and discussions."

"Are his friends?"

Aidan laughed. "Yes, he has some rabble-rousers among his associates. Makes one wonder why they keep him in the group."

"They do because he is their leader," Bella said. "Aidan, you have been so busy doing the mundane activities for the Duke you do not see what he really does! Consider where his study was when his children were little—on the same floor as their nursery, where he could watch over them and the staff taking care of them. What absent-minded academic does that? What peer does that?

"And what about his insistence that his son represent him at social events? I'm sure he had a delightfully rambling explanation of why this had to be, when in truth, it is so Lord Lakehurst might find his future wife. He knows that, with his writer's temperament, Lord Lakehurst would be more inclined to stay home and

write, versus socializing, especially given the fantastic
stories he writes. I am in awe of the cleverness of your
brother. I'm surprised your mother hasn't taken him
into hand yet. The man should remarry."

Aidan laughed. "That won't happen!"

"Maybe not, but it should. But we are not talking
of the Duke. We are talking of you, Aidan. I am hoping
we may be friends. You deserve the happiness I see
others in your family have found. There is no reason
you should be different from the others."

"I've missed you, Bella," Aidan said suddenly.
"Even when I hated you, I missed you."

She looked away for a moment, then looked back
at him. "As have I, you," she confessed. "But Aidan, we
are not the people we were three years ago. It is time
both of us looked to our own happiness, unfettered
from outside influences. I hope we can support each
other in this."

Aidan gazed at her. His heart had not changed. He
thought he loved her more now, loved the woman she
had become more than the girl he'd courted. He took
a deep, silent breath. "Yes, we can," he softly said.
Then, briskly, "We'd best find Mr. Martin and see
what he wants to do next, and tell him about your
finding."

"Yes."

Together, they walked back to the terrace, where
they found Mr. Martin inspecting the area around the
bench.

"Nothing to find around here," Mr. Martin told
them as they walked up the steps. "Your brother's servants were evidently quite efficient this morning," he
said, pointing to the scrubbed and swept terrace.

"Yes, but Lady Blessingame found something the
servants haven't cleaned up yet," Nowlton said.

Mr. Martin looked at her.

"This way," Bella said, leading him to the door that led into the Lady Margaret Parlor. "Lady Malmsby had not wanted to encourage use of this room, so they kept it dark and closed last night." She opened the door. "You will notice, Mr. Martin, how quiet the door is. Now look at the floor beyond the door."

Mr. Martin squatted down to better look at the outside debris now in the room.

"This is my mother's favorite room," Aidan said. "She is particular about how this room is kept up."

"But this room has not been cleaned," Mr. Martin stated.

"It shouldn't have needed a cleaning if no one came in it during the ball."

"Yes, I see what you mean."

From the music room came the strains of a violin.

"Who's playing the violin?" Mr. Martin asked.

"That would be Lady Guinevere."

"Your niece?"

"Yes."

"I don't believe I've met her yet. She arranged for the musicians, correct?" Mr. Martin asked.

"Yes. Would you like to meet her?"

"I'd like to meet everyone in the household. I'll need to meet these musicians of hers, as well."

"We will start with Gwinnie, then. That is the family pet name for her," he explained. "She won't mind being interrupted."

Aidan led them through the parlor and across the hall to the music room. He opened the door. "Excuse the interruption, Gwinnie. I'd like you to meet—"

"Lewis!" exclaimed Gwinnie.

Bella looked between them. A delighted smile

claimed Mr. Martin's face, while Gwinnie's face turned as red as her hair.

"You know each other?" Aidan asked.

Mr. Martin stood silently, looking for Gwinnie to answer.

"Yes, yes we do," Gwinnie said. "Through my charity work, isn't that right, Mr. Martin?"

Bella compressed her lips against a laugh as she watched their interaction. The situation definitely discomfited Gwinnie. It appeared Mr. Martin, like Mr. Hargate, had not known her real name. Fascinating. What exactly did Gwinnie do that she had met both a solicitor and a Bow Street Runner, under an assumed name?

"Yes. At...at...." He snapped his fingers. "Help me here, the name escapes me, at..."

"At Mrs. Southerlands'."

"Yes, thank you. I don't know why I couldn't remember the woman's name," he said with a smile.

"But you called him by his first name," Aidan said to Gwinnie, frowning.

"Did I?" Gwinnie said. "That is probably because that is what Mrs. Southerlands calls him. Never Mr. Martin. Always Lewis this and Lewis that."

"My lady, I did not know you play an instrument. Do you play the pianoforte as well as the violin?" he asked, walking over to the pianoforte. He struck a few chords and nodded. "It has a pleasant sound."

Bella recognized his action as a diversion from further questions. Now she really was curious as to Gwinnie's charity activities.

"Yes, I do," Gwinnie said, joining him by the instrument, "though I prefer the violin."

"I do like the pianoforte, though it has been a few years since I've played," Mr. Martin said.

"Does the Duke know about your charity work?" Aidan asked, trying to pull the conversation back.

Gwinnie flounced, her hand on her hip. "Yes, of course," Gwinnie said, scowling at her uncle.

Bella spoke up. "I cannot fathom how you manage to do so much!" she said. "You have your music, which I have heard you practice for hours, alone and with your ensemble—then there are your concerts, and your charity work!"

Bella turned toward Aidan. "Mr. Nowlton, your niece is an absolute wonder. I am in awe. Simply in awe. But what are we doing talking music and charities when we should discuss the shooting? Mr. Nowlton, I suggest we leave Mr. Martin to talk to Gwinnie, while we find Lord Lakehurst, so Mr. Martin can speak with him next."

"My ensemble group will be here soon for practice. We have a concert tonight in the Argyll Rooms, so it is best Mr. Martin and I speak now," Gwinnie said, smiling brightly at her uncle as Bella led him out of the room.

Aidan still frowned, but allowed himself to be escorted away. At the doorway to the main hall, he stopped and looked back at them standing by the pianoforte. "I will leave the door open," he said.

Mr. Martin smiled his crooked smile. "Of course."

～

"What was going on in there," Aidan asked, as they walked away from the music room and took the stairs to the first floor.

"Gwinnie is not known as Lady Guinevere Nowlton when she goes about her charity work. She does not want to appear like many society women do, granting favors to the lower classes, but never dirtying the hem of their dresses. She wants to genuinely help, and to do that, she works incognito. I assume she met Mt. Martin in her charity volunteer role."

"Why was I not told of this?"

"Why should you be?"

"Because I—" He stopped. "The family needs me to do the things I do. And for that, I have to know what is going on. My family are artists. They don't have their feet on the ground. I have my feet on the ground, and I do for them those things they would not know how to go about doing."

Bella emphatically shook her head. "I've listened to your family talk. They take for granted what you do for them. They think it's wonderful, they say it was something you developed as a small boy, asking what you can help with and have continued to this day. They believe it's what you like, so they find things for you to do for them, but they don't *need* you to do them."

Aidan looked at her, his brows furrowed. "I'm not talented like the rest of the family."

"That is not true," Bella protested, stopping in the middle of the stairs, forcing Aidan to stop as well.

"Bella, they have unique talents. I showed no signs of a talent that my parents could have—and would have—nurtured. They always encouraged me to try different things, and that is part of why I helped the others, thinking maybe I would find my niche. I never did."

Bella laughed. "Yes, you did." Her eyes danced. "You are a successful gallery owner."

Aidan rolled his eyes.

"What made you successful?" Bella persisted, climbing the stairs again.

"My family's position in society. I have no illusions about that."

"I will grant that was a contributing factor for society to seek you out," Bella said. "But your family connection wouldn't have lasted if you didn't have a critical eye for art."

"I have merely used what my mother taught me," he said.

"She may have encouraged you to like art, but you take it beyond that. You *understand* art. Others don't have an eye for the art aesthetic that you do. You see the art inside yourself. You feel it," she said earnestly. "Even Harry saw that. You can discern a technically competent piece from a brilliant piece.—And Lady Malmsby depends on you for that talent."

Aidan's lips twisted as he thought about that. He shook his head. "I will consider your words; however, I feel you are only being kind."

"*Kind*?" Bella protested, her voice rising. "No, I am telling you what I see. And I'm telling you, as loving as your family is, they are using you to deal with things they don't want to do."

Aidan compressed his lips, not responding. They had reached the old nursery and ballroom floor. He turned toward the nursery wing.

"Lake's writing eyrie, as he calls it, is the former governess's room," he said as they reached the old nursery. The door stood open.

Bella couldn't help but smile as they crossed the threshold to see child-height tables and chairs, books, long-forgotten toys, and small chalkboards still in the room. It was obvious the room continued to be maintained by the staff long since its use. There was no dust anywhere, and light streamed in clean windows.

"The governess room is over here," Aidan said, leading Bella to a door across the room.

Aidan knocked on the door.

"Wait!" The curt order came from within the room.

Aidan lounged against the door frame. "We could be here moments, or up to half an hour," he told Bella.

"How exceedingly rude," she said, frowning. "Even for the son of a duke!"

"No. If his muse is talking to him, he puts off visitors to finish a thought or a scene, so he doesn't lose the threads of the story that is in his head. When he finishes, he will open the door. This is why I wanted to warn him before Mr. Martin comes to talk to him."

When the door opened a few moments later, Lord Lakehurst's appearance quite surprised her. Shirt sleeves rolled up, no cravat, ink-stained fingers, the beginnings of a red beard shadowing his face, and his wavy dark-red hair standing on end in all directions. She blinked. "Lord Lakehurst," she said, inclining her head.

"None of that, Lady Blessingame. I'm Anonymous when I write," he declared, a cheeky grin lighting the large man's face.

"His pseudonym," Aidan explained drily. He straightened. "Mr. Martin is talking to Gwinnie right now."

A large, long-haired black cat with sleepy gold eyes sauntered to the door and looked up at them, his tail swishing.

"Hello, Oscar," Aidan said. He reached down to give the cat a quick pet, then looked back at Lord Lakehurst. "Mr. Martin will want to talk to you next."

Lord Lakehurst made a face. "Dashed bloody

bother—please excuse my language, Lady Blessingame," he said, his face turning red.

Bella compressed her lips against a laugh at his expression. "It is all right, Lord Lakehurst. Being in diplomatic service, that is mild to what I have heard."

"I appreciate your forbearance." He looked up and Aidan. "I suppose I should get cleaned up and civilized."

"I don't think Mr. Martin will pay the least bit of attention to your attire."

"No. He shan't, most likely. However, I will."

Bella and Aidan stepped back as Lake came out of his writing room. He looked back at the cat. "In or out?" he asked.

The cat sauntered out, then crossed the governess room and went out the open door. Lord Lakehurst shut the door behind him. "I'll go to my rooms to clean up. Where is he interrogating us?"

"Don't think of it as an interrogation," protested Bella.

"But it is! We are all suspects. He has to approach it that way," Lord Lakehurst said boisterously. "So, where do I go to meet him? I might get some excellent material for a book out of this."

"What about the Duke's old study on this floor?" Bella suggested.

"Excellent, then as soon as I'm done, I can get back to my writing," he said.

"Can I ask you, was that your cat?" Bella asked.

"Oscar? Yes. He is my writing muse, when he is in the mood, independent creature that he is. Since I write Gothics, I thought a black cat a suitable companion. Ha! A dog is a companion. A cat? A cat is whatever they wish to be, whenever they wish to be it."

"And with Oscar, it varies," put in Aidan with a laugh.

"Always," Lord Lakehurst said ruefully. He strode away from them, whistling.

Bella watched him bounce down the stairs and shook her head. "When I met him at dinner, the first night I arrived, he was quite formal and also at the ball last night."

Aidan nodded. "He is reserved around strangers. This is the real Lord Lakehurst. He must feel comfortable around you," Aidan said. "Now to tell the Duke and my mother."

"What about the servants—won't Mr. Martin want to interview them as well?"

"Yes, but we'll see to the family first. Mr. Harold can arrange the interviews with the rest of the staff, as he's already interviewed Jimmy."

"Where will the Duke be at this time? In his current study on the first floor?" Bella asked.

"Yes. Typically, he's gone after breakfast for his studies. I asked him to remain here today."

"Wouldn't he want to be here for the investigation?" Bella asked.

"He trusts me to take care of such matters for him."

Bella frowned. "This is what I meant about taking advantage of you."

"Bella, he is too much of an academic to pay attention to everyday situations," Aidan explained.

She kept silent a moment, wondering if she should reveal her conversation with the Duke. If he didn't want others to know, he shouldn't tell anyone. She decided he must feel the prank has gone on long enough, and that was why he was honest with her.

"No, he is not," she finally said. "While Lady

Malmsby may like jokes and pranks, his grace has been perpetuating the longest running prank and none of you have caught on."

"Malmsby? No," Aidan rejected her statement.

"Yes. He told me. He thinks it a lark that no one has asked him about his studies in years. Everyone assumes he is still deep in research on King Arthur," Bella said. "He's not. He told me he hasn't been since his wife died."

She saw the doubt in Aidan's face. "This is what I suggest you do. The next time you see your brother reading, ask him what he is reading. The next time he says he will be out for the day, ask him where he will be."

"I have asked after him from the servants when he wasn't around, and the answer I get is he is at the library."

"That's because he has requested that they lie for him."

"Then he'd probably lie to me as well."

"No, I don't believe he will. He wants to see if anyone is at all curious about what he does." She laughed. "As I think on it, the entire Nowlton family makes assumptions about each other all the time and you don't talk to each other. Rather sad, don't you agree?"

He looked at her quizzically but didn't answer.

He knocked on the Duke's study door.

"Enter."

Aidan pushed open the study door and bade Bella enter before him.

Like the old study upstairs, the room was bright, but it was not as big. Instead of two wing chairs, there was a leather sofa with a fur blanket thrown over the back. Guest chairs were more utilitarian than fashionable.

The Duke sat behind his desk, an open book, paper, pen, ink, and a cup of coffee on the desk before him. He closed the book and leaned back as they entered.

"Mr. Martin is here and has started his interviewing," Aidan told him.

His brother nodded. "Good. The sooner this gets resolved, the better."

"He'll want to interview you as well."

The Duke nodded. "As you requested, I am not going anywhere today—though this evening I would like to attend a lecture."

Aidan glanced at Bella, then looked back at his brother. "What kind of lecture?" Aidan asked.

His brother's lips twisted into a smirk as he looked over his glasses at Bella, then looked back at Aidan. "A lecture on the potential future of steam power for modern farm equipment," he said.

Bella smiled at the Duke. The Duke winked back.

Aidan looked between them. "And the book you're reading?"

"Oh, this?" his brother said casually. "It's a treatise on how steam power works. Thought I'd read up on that before tonight's lecture."

Aidan frowned. "No Arthurian work or other British mythos?"

The Duke shook his head. "My interests have turned to the sciences. I have particular interests in new discoveries that can lead to investment opportunity."

"That is a substantial change from King Arthur legends to science," Aidan protested.

His brother nodded and sadly smiled. "I know," he

admitted. "But I only pursued King Arthur because of Morgana. She had the fascination but could not do the research, as women are not allowed access to the resources. She was the love of my life, and I would do anything for her," he admitted, smiling at his memories.

"Including becoming an Arthurian scholar?"

"Yes. I miss her dearly, but after she died, I had no reason to continue with King Arthur, and honestly, contrary to Morgana's beliefs, I believe he is only a legend. So, after she died, I pursued my own interests."

"Why did you allow us to continue to believe you were researching King Arthur?"

The Duke shrugged. "Why not? No one was interested in King Arthur, so no one asked me questions. You left me alone, which I like."

"But you told Lady Blessingame," Aidan pointed out.

"Yes," his brother admitted. He leaned forward, entwining his fingers together on his desk. "I knew telling her would circle back to others in the family. Better than me suddenly confessing, was my thought. Also, might make everyone feel guilty that they never asked what I'm doing."

Aidan's brow furrowed. "Do you know Gwinnie is involved in charity work, and she does it under another name?"

The Duke sat straighter at his desk. "As Sarah Knolls? Yes, I do."

"Why wasn't I told?" Aidan asked. "I would have liked to watch out for her safety."

The Duke shrugged. "There was no need. I discussed her safety with the Earl of Soothcoor, and he assured me he would discretely arrange for someone to watch over her."

Aidan didn't know how he felt about his brother's revelation that he had done something without consulting him or asking him to do it. In one way, he was glad he hadn't known it. That would have been one more responsibility for him to navigate for his family, and lately he'd been feeling the mounting burden. In another, he admitted to feeling piqued that they left him out. Confounding.

Bella laughed. "I'd wager the gentlemen the Earl asked are Mr. Hargate and Mr. Martin. He assigned them the task of watching over the welfare of a Miss Sarah Knolls without telling them who she was!" she exclaimed. "That is how they both recognized her."

The Duke nodded. "He mentioned a Hargate and a Martin. I don't know Mr. Hargate— however, I assume Mr. Martin is the Bow Street Runner my mother sent for?"

"Yes, he is," said Aidan.

"Mr. Hargate is a solicitor," Bella supplied. "Of Hargate, Owen, and Hargate."

"The solicitors you met with two days ago, the ones who gave you the letters?" Aidan asked.

"Yes. Mr. Hargate senior was Harry's solicitor. Do you think Mr. Martin is done interviewing Gwinnie?" Bella asked. "Lake should be ready and waiting."

"Where are Mr. Martin and Lake to meet?"

"I told Lord Lakehurst that your old study would work."

The Duke nodded. "Think I'll go up and join them," he said, rising.

CHAPTER 10

OSCAR

As they all left the Duke's study, they heard music.

"Gwinnie's ensemble is here," said the Duke.

Aidan nodded. "She said they would come today to practice. We thought that fortuitous, as Mr. Martin could interview them while they're here."

"Oh, yes, they were in attendance as well. Of course! Maybe I am at times an absent-minded academic," the Duke joked.

"I hear a pianoforte. I thought her keyboardist was not available because of an injury," Aidan mused.

"That is what she told me as well," said Bella.

"I wonder who is playing?" the Duke said. "I'm curious. I think I will come with you, instead."

From the door of the music room, they saw the Spaniard playing the flute and Mr. Martin playing the pianoforte! It sounded like they were having a music duel. Enchanted by their music, Bella clasped her hands to her chest, her eyes bright.

It appeared neither man felt enchanted with the other. Their expressions were solemn as they played fiercely on their instruments. Gwinnie stood next to the pianoforte, bouncing excitedly on her toes. The other musicians were bobbing in their chairs or toe-tapping.

Bella, Aidan, and the Duke came further into the room. Bella sat down on the edge of a chair to listen. How does a Bow Street agent learn to play the pianoforte so well?

Aidan leaned over to whisper in Bella's ear. "Another surprise," he whispered.

Bella nodded as Mr. Martin broke off playing. The Spaniard awkwardly stopped as well.

"My apologies," Aidan said. "I didn't mean for you to stop."

Mr. Martin rubbed his palms along his pant legs. "I needed to stop. I have more people to interview today." He rose from the pianoforte bench and bowed toward the Spaniard.

"Thank you, Don Joaquín Pedroso y Castel. Well played," he said.

The don's lip curled at the corner as he bowed his acknowledgment and salute to his opponent. He eased himself down in his chair, extending his bad leg out before him.

"Have you interviewed the musicians already?" Aidan asked Mr. Martin.

"Yes. Musicians always have interesting observations about the surrounding people. Very productive. Thank you all."

"Lord Malmsby, this is Mr. Lewis Martin from Bow Street. Martin, this is my brother, his grace, the Duke of Malmsby."

Mr. Martin bowed to Lord Malmsby, who waved aside that action. "Please, no."

"Lord Lakehurst is meeting you in the Duke's old study," Aidan told him.

"I'll show him the way," the Duke said, "so he can interview us both."

"We'll leave you and your associates alone now." Aidan told Gwinnie. "See you at dinner?" He opened the music room door. Oscar darted into the room.

"Yes. And I shall want to hear all about the day," Gwinnie said. "No, Oscar! Out!" she told the cat, trying to shoo him back out the door.

"Our bass player, Mr. Sumptner, is terribly allergic," Gwinnie explained. "Can you help get Oscar out?" she requested.

Oscar had taken a seated position in front of the musicians, a concert attendee awaiting a performance. Oscar mildly growled as Aidan picked him up. As he straightened, Aidan was curious as to the expression on the Spaniard's face. While Mr. Sumptner might be allergic, the Spaniard looked terrified. He made the sign of the cross.

"Might I hold him?" Bella asked. "Will he let me?" She held out her arms.

Aidan laughed. "Yes. Oscar loves attention." He handed him to her, then looked back at Gwinnie. "Dinner should prove interesting tonight. We will have some revelations for you," he promised.

She nodded, thanked them for removing the cat, then turned back to her musicians. Aidan closed the music room door softly behind them as they left.

❧

WITH THE DOOR to the music room closed behind them, Oscar squirmed in Bella's arms to be let down. Bella laughed, but let him down and watched as the cat ran down the hall and up the stairs.

"You go with the Duke," Bella suggested to Aidan

after the cat ran out of sight. She looked back at him. "I'll sit with the Duchess until Mr. Martin is through talking to Lord Lakehurst and the Duke. Then you can escort Mr. Martin here for her interview."

Aidan nodded. "She would be more comfortable in her own domain."

"It will probably be teatime by then anyway," Bella ruefully said.

Aidan smiled. "Wouldn't want to disrupt Mother's tea," he said. "I will see you later then. And Bella—"

"Yes?"

"I think you are correct. We can be friends."

She smiled back at him. "Yes," she said. She turned to walk across the hall to the Lady Margaret Parlor.

Aidan watched her go. *And maybe more?*

"BELLA!" Lady Malmsby said when she saw her in the doorway. She laid aside the book she'd been reading and swung her legs from the sofa to the floor. "Come, come sit by me. I feel there is much to discuss."

Bella crossed the room to sit by Lady Malmsby.

Lady Malmsby took Bella's hands in hers. "You, dear child, have had an eventful few days since you came to stay here. Perhaps you would have been better staying at Mivart's Hotel!"

Bella shook her head. "No, no, not at all. I would have gone to the solicitor's by myself. The information they passed to me was overwhelming. I should have been quite undone."

"I doubt that," said Lady Malmsby. "You are a re-sourceful, strong woman. And consider, Lord Candel-stone might not be with us now if you hadn't rushed to stem his loss of blood."

Bella demurred.

"Well, luckily we will never know," Lady Malmsby said. "What I want to tell you about is the discussion I had with Lord Malmsby this morning." She shook her head, silver-gray curls bouncing slightly. "I thought I knew my son. I was vastly mistaken... He will have private conversations with a couple of the cabinet members to suggest a foreign mission for Candelstone that will get him out of the country for at least a year. He said there is support in the government for Candelstone's intent to suppress these riots against machines. For one, Lord Castlereagh is a supporter."

"Oh, dear," Bella said.

"Yes. There is, however, agreement that Candelstone's methods need... well, *adjusting* was the word Malmsby used. He says Candelstone has leaped to fill a void. He will suggest that sending Candelstone away for a year will allow them to put people in place to control these riots who are not fanatics like Candelstone."

"But where would they send him that he wouldn't cause issues?" Bella asked.

"He told me Lord Liverpool and some others have received requests from a gentleman from the South Americas, who has asked for help from England. His name is Simón Bolívar."

"I have not heard of him," Bella admitted.

"I believe I saw him mentioned in a newspaper regarding Spain taking back New Granada last year. This gentleman is in the Caribbean at the moment. He has been fighting to free the South and Central Americas from Spanish rule, and has pledged to ensure they outlaw slavery in these areas if he is victorious."

"That is certainly an incentive," Bella said.

"Malmsby tells me there are many reasons for

England to wish him success, but we can't enter into another war right now, particularly with Spain, an ally. We do need to know more about this Bolívar gentleman, however. Malmsby is proposing sending Candelstone to investigate Bolívar and get a firsthand idea of what is going on in that part of the world. We will want to know if his actions could negatively impact our colonies in the area."

Bella considered the idea. Then she smiled. "It might answer."

"I did not know Lord Malmsby was so knowledgeable about politics. He never talks politics, though I know he takes his duty to the House of Lords seriously," Lady Malmsby said.

"Did he tell you he no longer researches or writes about King Arthur?" Bella asked.

"He did. I was shocked."

"I think he out pranked you, your grace, keeping his change in interests and activities secret."

Lady Malmsby blinked, then laughed. "Yes, he certainly has! And I love that. He has certainly put me on my mettle."

CHAPTER 11

TEA

B ella was in a calm frame of mind by the time the maid arrived with tea. She and the Duchess talked of fashion, upcoming weddings, and the unusually cool and rainy weather. By unspoken agreement, they chose not to speak of the shooting or Bella's revelations concerning Sir Harry. Bella welcomed the diversion and silently blessed the Duchess for her wisdom.

Close behind the maid came the gentlemen, and Bella knew her peace to be at an end.

"Have you solved the mystery amongst you?" Lady Malmsby half-humorously asked as they entered. She signaled to the maid that she could serve.

The Duke shook his head. "And we have gone over the guest list with Mr. Martin."

"What about that young man who was first out the door? I remember where I've seen him before. My brother pointed him out to me at the RA. Andrew told me his name is Reggie Stafford. He said he used to be Candelstone's secretary, and has had a hard time finding another suitable position after Lord Candelstone abruptly retired," Bella said. "He might have some animosity for Lord Candelstone," she said, as she accepted a cup of tea from the maid.

"In that case, Lord Candelstone would be the intended victim, not the substitute as Lord Candelstone has alluded." Mr. Martin said.

"Reginald Stafford? Baron Stafford's youngest boy?" asked Lady Malmsby. "I saw him on the stairs as I heard the gunshot. It couldn't have been him."

"Could someone gain entrance to the ball who wasn't on the guest list?" Mr. Martin asked.

"It's possible," the Duke admitted.

Mr. Martin nodded as he picked up his teacup, then looked at the Duchess. "You grace, please tell me what you remember from last evening," he said, before he sipped his tea.

She shrugged. "It was like any other ball. Lots of people to talk to, lots of gossip flowing. I had made one round of the ballroom. Took me about an hour, as there were so many people to greet, and spinsters and wallflowers to introduce to eligible gentlemen for a dance. Then, of course, ensuring the staff were watching over the refreshments and no young bucks adding more spirits to the punch bowl."

"Has that happened before?" Mr. Martin asked.

"What?"

"Guests adding more alcohol to the punch."

Lady Malmsby laughed. "Yes. Oh, yes—though not for many years. It was near time for the first supper seating and some guests were gathering near the ballroom entrance to go downstairs upon Mr. Harold's announcement. I remember the Spaniard left the other musicians as they played a last piece before they took a break. He walked slowly, leaning on his cane. I wondered at his pain for standing so long as he played his flute. Gwinnie had arranged food and drinks for them in the small guest parlor next to this one," she said, pointing toward the front of the house.

"When Mr. Harold announced the first seating, I watched the people go down the stairs. Bella, I saw your brother, then. He was escorting Miss Beddlington downstairs. They appeared to be discoursing easily together."

"They have known each other for many years. I think she has given up on him coming up to scratch. My brother is oblivious. She is probably a good match for him. She is sweet, but not overly bright."

Lady Malmsby ruefully smiled and nodded in understanding.

"Had Captain Melville reached the bottom of the stairs when you heard the gunshot?" Mr. Martin asked.

"I don't believe so," Lady Malmsby said.

"Thank you, your grace," Mr. Martin said. He set down his teacup and turned to Lady Blessingame. "My lady, are you ready to tell me about your actions from last evening?"

"Yes."

"I understand from Mr. Nowlton that you had words with Lord Candelstone last night."

She nodded. "Yes, much the same as you saw this morning in his room. He wants me to return to doing cryptography work, and I do not wish to do that. I feel he is searching for some lever to use to force my compliance. He does not believe I mean *No*. I told him to leave me alone."

She put her teacup down and sat straighter. She stared off across the room, unseeing.

"I decided Mr. Nowlton needed to learn we had been misled and lied to three years ago, and we shouldn't blame each other for what occurred. We had words on the ballroom floor, which I'm sure people saw, then I drew him away to talk privately in the Duke's old study, where you were this afternoon with Lord Lakehurst and the Duke. I had left the letters I received from the solicitor in that room and I showed them to him, asking for him to read them. He didn't want to believe me—"

"It wasn't that," protested Aidan.

"Yes, it was," Bella said, glancing at him. "Ignorance was—in many ways—less painful than the truth for either of us. We were coming to terms in our discussion when my brother burst into the room, expecting to find an orgy."

"Oh, surely not!" protested Lady Malmsby, laughing a little.

"I think he did, being Andrew," Bella said with a shrug. "When I found out Lord Candelstone had sent him to find me, my anger ignited fireworks. I came at him and pushed him. I 'm ashamed to admit I might have slapped him if he hadn't caught my hands. I was that angry. When he stopped me, my emotions overwhelmed me and I burst into tears and threw myself back in the chair. No matter what I did, Lord Candelstone has somehow been there to ruin my peace."

"It was when I saw Lord Candelstone would not let up on Bella that I knew she hadn't lied. I vowed then to get Candelstone out of her life," Aidan told the others.

"I told Captain Melville to stay with her until I could send someone to her. He was told to not speak to her. To just be there. I came back to the ballroom and found Gwinnie. I asked her to go to Lady Blessingame and stay with her until I returned."

"And that is when you went in search of your brother-in-law, as you related earlier to me?"

"Yes."

"Lady Blessingame, what did you do? You did not stay in that room, did you?"

"No. I felt I wanted—no, I *needed*—to calm down." Bella paused. "I had cried too many tears over the past two days. The memories made me cry, and I needed to rise above them. I refuse to be chattel to my past," she said decisively. She took a deep breath. "I took the servants' stairway to the ground floor to walk in the garden, thinking fresh air would revive me. And it did. I didn't see anything out in the garden save for a cat slinking among the bushes. I think it was Oscar. I stopped by the fountain and looked up at the stars, willing my body and soul to calm. Then I heard the gunshot."

"You didn't see anyone or anything out of the ordinary in the garden."

She shook her head. "Nothing."

"What time do you think this was?"

Bella laughed shortly. "I do not know. All I can say is what others have said, and only because I have heard them say it."

"What did you do when you heard the gunshot?"

"I crouched down, and then ran as fast as I could in that position back to the terrace steps."

"Why did you crouch down?" Aidan asked.

Bella shrugged with her hands as she smiled wryly. "That's what Harry said to do when I hear gunfire."

"That sounds like an appropriate action," said Lady Malmsby. She clasped her hands in her lap.

"Then what?" Mr. Martin encouraged.

I ran up the terrace steps and looked all about. There were people leaning out the ballroom balcony windows.

I asked them if they could see anything. One woman pointed to an area in shadows at the other end of the terrace. I ran to that area and found Lord Candelstone. He was still a little conscious but couldn't tell me anything. I pressed my hands tight against his chest to slow the loss of blood. I didn't know if it would help or not, but it was the only thing I knew to do. He was bleeding heavily. At least it seemed so to me. The first person to come up to me was Reggie Stafford. He was useless. Mr. Nowlton pushed him aside and started ordering everyone about. Then Dr. Nowlton came up and told us what to do. Afterward, Mr. Nowlton escorted me to the bench. The blood had soaked my gloves, so I stripped them off and dropped them to the ground." She picked up her teacup for another sip before continuing.

"Then Ellinbourne and Ann came up to see how I was. After talking to them, I decided to go to my room. I leaned down to pick up the gloves, and that is when I felt something lying next to the gloves. I pulled it out, and it was a muff pistol. I gave it to Ellinbourne, then I went upstairs by the servants' stairway."

"You didn't see anyone else?"

"No, nothing."

"This morning you pointed out dirt and broken leaves inside this room. How was it you came to see those?

"I was looking for her grace. I thought she might be here. She wasn't, but I came in anyway. I looked out the windows and saw how clean the terrace looked. I walked closer, marveling at how tranquil it appeared outside. The servants had cleansed the terrace so no evidence of what occurred last night remained. I turned away and happened to glance down. That's when I saw those bits of debris on the floor. At first, it amused me to see the servants had cleaned the outside but not the inside. Then I recalled no one was supposed to be in this room last night, so there was no reason for it to be cleaned this morning. I thought about what that might mean, so I showed it to you and Mr. Nowlton."

"You didn't open the door?"

"No. When Mr. Nowlton and I went out, we went out through the hall door. The door wasn't opened until we saw you."

"Thank you, Lady Blessingame." Mr. Martin jotted some additional notes in his occurrence book. Afterward, he closed the book and stuck it into his waistcoat pocket. "I'm going to be going now. I want to interview guests and do an investigation on that gun —on the chance I can find the dealer in London familiar with the weapon and who might have purchased it."

The door to the Lady Margaret Parlor opened and Gwinnie entered.

"All done with the practice for today?" Lady Malmsby asked Gwinnie.

"Yes, since we are playing at the Argyll Rooms this evening, we ended practice early. The others have left, except for Don Joaquín—he's copying a piece of music I have. I've asked him to join us for dinner, then he and I can go on to the venue afterword."

"I'll be there tonight," Lady Malmsby said. "I'm joining Lady Oakley and Mr. Rutherford."

"Splendid!" Gwinnie said. "Will you come too, Bella?" Gwinnie asked.

"Not tonight. Mr. Nowlton invited Andrew for breakfast this morning, but my brother sent a note saying he wouldn't be able to make it. He said he would come by to speak with me this evening. He is certain I am going to be arrested for shooting Lord Candelstone."

Mr. Martin frowned. "Why would your brother assume you would be arrested?"

Bella sighed. "He heard some guests suggest I shot Lord Candelstone, as they saw me next to him. He assumed that was the truth."

"Captain Melville is a gullible man—sparing Lady Blessingame's familial feelings—that is the kindest way I have to describe Melville," Nowlton explained dryly.

Mr. Martin suppressed a laugh.

Bella frowned at Mr. Nowlton, but she couldn't naysay his words because they were true. Andrew was gullible.

Mr. Martin rose. "Do you have plans for tomorrow, in case I need to speak with you further?" he asked, looking about the room at the others.

Lord Lakehurst said he would be writing, and the Duke said he was going to a scientific demonstration.

"I'll stay close to the gallery," Aidan told him, "So I can be available whenever you like."

"Gwinnie and I are going to Richmond tomorrow," Bella said.

"That is right, you have an appointment to see your new home," Lady Malmsby said. "I believe I will accompany you, if you don't believe you will need me for anything more tomorrow, Mr. Martin?"

Mr. Martin bowed to her. "Not at all, your grace."

"That would be wonderful to have you with us," Bella said.

"I'll ask Cook to arrange a picnic for us," Lady Malmsby suggested. "We shall make a day of it. I think we deserve it."

Gwinnie nodded.

Bella clapped her hands together. "I should very much like that, after the events of the past two days."

Mr. Martin bowed to them all and left.

Lady Malmsby rose, and the others rose as well. "I believe I will lie down before dinner," she announced. "Oh, dash it. I suppose I should check on Silly Willy as well. Hmm, and maybe guilt Catherine into joining us for dinner instead of staying cooped in her bedroom suite of rooms."

The others laughed and nodded as Lady Malmsby led them out of the room.

LIVELINESS AT DINNER gladdened Bella's heart. Beside Don Joaquín joining the family, the Duchess had convinced Lady Catherine to attend, and Ann, Mrs. Hallowell, and the Duke of Ellinbourne were also in attendance. As Ann said, coming to dinner was the best way to find out the latest news regarding the shooting. And it was, for that topic of conversation was on everyone's tongue.

"Merlin, how is your patient?" the Duke asked his son.

"Doing quite well. Perhaps not as well as he thinks he is doing. He is determined to quit his bed on the morrow."

"Will you let him?" the Duke asked.

"I don't think I could stop him!" Merlin said.

"He is quite determined," added Lady Catherine. "He sent out letters to his associates, asking them to visit him tomorrow, and he won't do that from his bed."

The Duke grunted acknowledgment. He forked another bit of quail. "Mother, the sauce on this quail is superb," he said, before raising the food to his mouth.

"Oh, you notice what you are eating? That's new," teased Gwinnie. "If Grandmother had not brought her chef with her, we would eat bland boiled beef and potatoes without sauce," she told the company.

The company laughed.

"Sadly true," Lord Lakehurst said. He reached for the salt cellar on the table before him at the same time the Don did, their hands colliding, spilling salt on the table.

Lord Lakehurst laughed.

"No! No! Do not laugh, my lord. You must quickly throw a pinch of the spilled salt over your shoulder like this," the Spaniard said, taking a pinch of the spilled salt and tossing it over his shoulder. "This blinds El Diablo. If you do not, he will try to trick you and bind you to him."

"I've never heard of that superstition. I could use that in one of my books," Lord Lakehurst said.

"My heart, it is racing. Please my lord, do this for me," the Don said earnestly, a sheen of sweat appearing on his forehead.

Everyone turned to the Spaniard, alarmed.

"Don Joaquín!" Gwinnie cried out. "Are you all right?" She searched his face earnestly.

"All right, all right. I will," Lord Lakehurst agreed, shrugging good-naturedly. He took a pinch of salt and threw it over his shoulder as the Don did.

"Thank you, my lord," said Don Joaquín, tapping his forehead with his handkerchief. The handkerchief showed small blotches of black. He quickly stuffed it back in his pocket.

"Your grace," Lady Catherine said suddenly, addressing Ellinbourne, who sat to her left. "Did you bring your sketchbook with you this evening?" she asked.

Ellinbourne smiled at her. "Yes, I did."

"After dinner, do you think I might see what you have drawn as others have?" she asked.

"Certainly. And perhaps you will allow me to do a sketch of you as well?"

"Oh! Oh!" She blushed. "That would be lovely," she said, casting her eyes down. "Thank you."

"Lady Blessingame," invited the Duke, "tell us about this property you have in Richmond."

"All I know is what the solicitors told Gwinnie and me. It was where Harry installed his mistresses until we married. At that time, Harry instructed the solicitors to lease out the house, and keep it leased for two years following his death."

"And to keep the property a secret from you until two years had passed?" Lord Lakehurst clarified.

Bella nodded. "That is what they told me."

"It has been over two years since Sir Harry died. Why has it taken them so long to contact you?" the Duke of Ellinbourne asked.

"Harry ordered work to be done on the house, repairs and modernization, none of which they could do until the tenants moved out."

"They told her the house is empty, ready for her to furnish and decorate as she pleases," Gwinnie said.

"Like a blank artist's canvas," observed Ellinbourne.

"Exactly. I'll own that sounds both a daunting and an intriguing proposition to me," Gwinnie said.

"That is how I feel," Bella admitted.

"Now I am glad I said I would go with you tomorrow to view the house," Lady Malmsby said.

"From the directions on the papers they gave me, it

doesn't appear to be far out, only just into Richmond," Bella said. "My original plan when coming to London was to find a property to lease that I could share with my brother Andrew. I'm hoping this house is not too far out for him to reside there and fulfill his duties to his regiment," she said.

"You are close to your brother," gentle Ann said sympathetically.

"Yes," Bella said with a smile. "He is not the smartest of fellows, but he is my brother and all I have. I have been watching out for him since we were children."

"Pardon, Lady Guinevere, but the time—" interrupted Don Joaquín.

Gwinnie looked at the marquetry clock on the grand fireplace mantel. "Yes! We should be going," she said, sliding her chair back.

"But we haven't had dessert yet," protested the Duchess. "And the concert is not for another hour-and-a-half."

"True—however, as the musicians, we have to be there early. We are a little later than we should be as it is," Gwinnie explained.

"All right then," said Lady Malmsby, looking forlorn, but resigned. "I look forward to seeing you later at the Argyll. Don Joaquín, thank you for joining us this evening."

"It has been a pleasure, your grace. Lady Blessingame, I wish you good luck with your new home." The Don bowed and followed Gwinnie out of the dining room.

~

LATER THAT EVENING, after her brother left, Bella returned to the Lady Margaret Parlor. She knew only herself, Lord Lakehurst in his writing eyrie, and the staff to be in the house. Ellinbourne had escorted Ann and Mrs. Hallowell back to their home. They'd only agreed to stay at Malmsby House until after the ball, so both were eager to once again sleep in their own rooms. Aidan—Mr. Nowlton, as she should refer to him—had returned to his townhouse, which housed his gallery on the ground floor and his living space above. The Duke went to his club to start his campaign for Candelstone's overseas assignment. Lady Malmsby and Gwinnie were yet at the Argyll rooms, and likely would be for another two hours.

She liked the quiet of the house, still restlessness made peace elude her. She wandered out of the Lady Margaret Parlor and down the white-and-black marble-tiled hall, her hand delicately trailing against furniture and statuary she passed.

"Did you need something, my lady?" asked the footman, as he rose from his shadowed seat by the front door. His sudden, shadowed presence made Bella's heart jump and race, but she swiftly recovered.

"No, no, nothing, thank you," she said softly as she turned to climb the red-and-gold carpeted stairs to the first floor.

"If you are needing a glass to fortify you, the library always has a bottle and glasses out," the now disembodied voice of the footman said, as she slowly climbed the stairs.

Bella turned back and flashed a smile in the footman's direction. "Thank you," she said. She climbed the stairs and turned toward the library, deciding the footman's suggestion had merit. It struck her as typical in the Nowlton family for the staff to feel comfortable to offer suggestions. She liked that.

Faint light glowed from under the heavy wood-paneled door. She hadn't been in this room; except for the first tour. A couple of oil lamps were lit, one on the beverage table.

Bella smiled. Keeping a lit lantern on the beverage table served as a testament to the footman's assurance of the bottle and glass available, complete with the ability to see what one was doing.

"The one on the right is brandy. The one on the left is port," said a man's voice from the vicinity of the fireplace. It was Lord Lakehurst.

Bella didn't jump at the sound of his voice. Though she had hoped to get her drink, then make her way up to her room where she could think about her brother's visit. Courtesy demanded otherwise.

Her brother had not been happy with her—gracious, he could whine like a toddler. She'd forgotten in the months since she last saw him how much hard work it could be to get him to listen to her, let alone understand her. He had been taught that gentlemen take care of the ladies, and he was determined to take care of his widowed sister in every wrong-headed way imaginable, and then some that weren't imaginable.

She knew he meant well. Still, he exhausted her. She was glad he said Richmond was too far out for him. After their conversation this evening, she didn't want to live with her brother.

But she didn't want to live alone either. She knew what her heart wanted. Her heart wanted to turn back the clock three years. She wanted Aidan Nowlton, the upright, overly formal gallery owner, whose sense of duty to his family led him to believe he needed to run his family's world. And she selfishly wanted him to herself.

She turned toward Lord Lakehurst. She could make out the dim shape of him reclining sideways, one leg over the upholstered chair arm. He sat backlit by a low fire in the fireplace.

"Do you have a recommendation, my lord?" Bella asked.

"Brandy," he said. "French brandy, well-aged, never paid a farthing to customs," he said, waving his glass before him.

Bella frowned. "Are you drunk, my lord?"

Lord Lakehurst laughed. "No, I haven't arrived at that state yet. I just entered this room not five minutes before you. Go ahead, pour yourself a glass, then come sit with me and we can solve the riddles of the world together."

Bella poured herself a glass of brandy, then went to sit in the facing chair to his. "So, what has you in the blue megrims, my lord," Bella asked as she sat down. She kicked off her slippers and tucked her feet under her as she relaxed in the chair.

"Do you want to know? Do you really want to know? I promised the manuscript to my publisher next week, and I don't know how the blasted book ends—and worse, this is not a problem I can ask Uncle Aidan to solve for me."

"You shouldn't have Uncle Aidan solve anything for you," Bella remonstrated, wondering if all men dropped into toddler behavior when thwarted in some way.

Lord Lakehurst straightened in his chair. "Ah-ha! The lady has feelings for said Uncle Aidan."

"Nonsense," Bella briskly lied. "What I have are eyes and ears, and I see how you all treat him."

Lord Lakehurst leaned back against the chair back. "And how do we treat him?" he asked.

"You depend on him to do anything you don't feel like handling. All the business-of-life things."

"Not true."

"Let me ask you a question, and we will see if I am right or wrong. When you decided you needed to find a publisher for your manuscript, what did you do?"

"I asked—oh!" He laughed. "All right, you have me on that one. I asked Aidan to find out about publishers for a Gothic romance," he admitted.

"If it is any consolation, everyone in your family does this. Who has taken charge of the investigation of the shooting? Who made the announcement to the guests last night? Why not the Duke whose house the incident occurred in, or you, his heir? You all assumed Aidan would take charge. And of course, he did. But why make that assumption?"

Lord Lakehurst spread his hands out. "Because he does?" he suggested.

"Not good enough," she said tersely, her lips compressing tightly.

Lord Lakehurst looked at her in the dim light. Then he smiled.

"We need you, Lady Blessingame," he told her.

"What?"

"The Malmsby dukedom needs you," he said. "The Nowlton family needs you. We are an odd lot, and somewhere along the way, we have lost our sense of worth."

"Lord Lakehurst, that is a powerful statement."

"Yes. But I think it is true. You have opened my eyes to our dependency. Do you realize it is almost a joke in the household to say *ask Aidan to do it*? We could say let the Duke's secretary do it, or the estate steward, or Mr. Harold, but more often than not, we do not. *Ask Aiden to do it* is what we say to each other," he said lightly.

Then one corner of his mouth quirked up. "You have made me realize that sometimes the expression that swiftly crosses his face is exasperation," he said seriously. "Why does he never complain or push back? I'm sure there are times he has other things he needs to do for his gallery, when instead he's trotting off on some request of ours that we or one of the staff might do."

"Doing things for others feels good. That is how it started for him. Now it is habit," Bella said.

"You need to marry Nowlton and keep him otherwise occupied," Lakehurst stated.

Bella laughed. "Why me?"

"Because he loves you," Lord Lakehurst said simply, with a slight shrug of his broad shoulders. He drained his glass in one swallow.

"You are confusing now with three years ago. I'm just hoping he can shed the hate for me he formed back then."

Lakehurst shook his head and waved a dismissive hand as he stood up. "That was gone immediately that he saw you. I can see that in how he looks at you. Pardon, my lady, but I must bid you adieu," he said with a flourishing bow. "I'm off to see if I can write a few more pages in this recalcitrant manuscript before sleep claims me."

"Goodnight, Lord Lakehurst," Bella replied, smiling at his theatrical parting.

Her smile dimmed as the door to the library closed behind him. She took another sip of the brandy, then set the glass on a table beside the chair.

She needed to think, and she didn't need brandy clouding her thoughts.

She got up to poke the fire, coaxing it to give out a little more heat before it settled into embers, then she sat back down, her feet tucked under her. She leaned her elbow on the armrest and cradled her chin in her hand.

Despite over a three-year separation, Bella admitted she had feelings for Aidan Nowlton, feelings that she strived to ignore, to deny. The effort was a vanity because of the embarrassment she harbored. A way to hide from her mistakes. She'd failed to believe in him when it counted the most. She'd failed him and herself. She did not want to pass blame to another. Yes, Harry had brilliantly set them up. She wanted to believe that love was greater than all the lies in the world.

Don't be an idealist, Bella, she told herself.

She was being nonsensical and knew it. Fear drove her. Fear that Aidan could never feel for her as she still felt for him. It was easier to deny than to open herself up to the possibility they might rekindle what they had before. If anything, she knew her love to be different. That she couldn't ignore or deny. She had changed, but so had he. There was more wisdom in her thoughts about him now. A grounded depth that burned greater than that young girl's love ever had. She must open herself up to the possibility. Stop automatically saying that the things Harry taught her now made her ineligible for love. She needed to get that straight in her head. She was worthy of love, no matter her past. The past was the past and today is today, she told herself fiercely, standing strong, looking toward all her tomorrows.

CHAPTER 12

HE LIED

When Nowlton entered the breakfast parlor at Malmsby House the next morning, he expected to find Lady Blessingame partaking of her breakfast. It disappointed him to discover she had already left for Richmond with his mother and Gwinnie. He'd hoped to have time to speak with her before she left. He'd done considerable thinking the night before, wandering through his empty townhouse. They had both changed in the intervening three years; however, not in any way to make them less likely to be attracted to each other. Quite the contrary. He found himself more intrigued by her now than he'd been three years ago. He didn't remember having an ache inside, crying out to hold her in his arms. He wanted to touch her, anywhere and everywhere. She espoused changes in her that barred their being able to get together. He disagreed. The changes only made the ties stronger.

He wanted to tell her all this, to beg her, if necessary, to give them a chance. He no longer wanted an empty townhouse. Though it had been his respite from the family's many asks, it no longer gave him a peace he craved. He craved companionship. He craved love. He craved Bella.

He hoped she didn't fall in love with her Richmond house. It was far from his gallery.

He picked at his breakfast in a desultory fashion until he heard a commotion out in the hall. He straightened to listen, then snorted. It was Lord Candelstone deciding to come downstairs, fussing at the attending footmen and his wife with every step down.

He should finish his breakfast quickly, else Lord Candelstone could give him stomach pains, he mused.

"Ah, Nowlton—good, you're here," said Candelstone, as he came into the breakfast parlor.

"Catherine told me something highly interesting from the dinner last night. Highly interesting. Wish I'd paid better attention at the ball," he said.

Nowlton glared up at Candelstone. "What are you talking about?"

"The shooter. My Catherine figured it out," he said. He grabbed his wife's hand and kissed her fingertips.

Lady Candelstone blushed and pulled her hand away.

"Top notch woman. Always has been. She knows make-up and disguise better than any Covent Garden performer or criminal denizen."

Lord Lakehurst entered the breakfast parlor followed by Lord Malmsby, "What are you carrying on about, Candelstone?" Malmsby asked.

"The shooter. It's Vizconde Miguel Carrasco-Torres!" he said with glee.

"Carrasco-Torres! Yesterday, you said Lady Blessingame killed him."

Candelstone squirmed a bit, his lips pursing. "So, I lied," he admitted. "I need her skills. The radicals that are threatening the country communicate in code. I need her to figure out their code."

"What does needing her skills have to do with lying?"

"Guilt. She feels guilty. I can work with that," he said sagely. "I can use that to get her to work with me."

Nowlton rose from his chair. He leaned forward, resting his knuckles on the table. "Listen to me, Candelstone," Nowlton said tersely, each word said distinctly. "Lady Blessingame will never work for you again."

Candelstone sneered as he scoffed, "Gallery owner."

"I'm not," said Malmsby. "And I agree with Aidan. Lady Blessingame will never work for you again."

Candelstone shook his head. "You are delusional. You think your title gives you any cachet to make that statement? Everyone knows you are an addle-pated academic. No one will listen to you."

"Are you quite certain about that?" Malmsby asked conversationally. He picked up his coffee cup. Blew on the hot brew a moment. "I sought out Lord Castlereagh last night. Discovered he's the person who has asked you to create a secret service to investigate and stop these radical groups before they become a problem. He's even secretly funding it." The Duke sipped his coffee.

"What?" Aidan and Lord Lakehurst exclaimed.

Candelstone smiled. "Yes. I don't know how you got that out of him, but that is true. And that is why I will have Lady Blessingame work with us. I have Lord Castlereagh's blessing on this."

The Duke shook his head. "Not anymore, you don't. Castlereagh can't afford to show his hand yet as to his attitude toward the radicals. Not everyone in government agrees to the need for an aggressive approach to these nascent anti-technology radical groups, thus the secret service."

Lord Lakehurst grinned as he dug into his rasher of ham.

Aidan relaxed back into his seat. He didn't know what his brother had done, but he had faith in him. He hadn't seen that canny expression on his face since he was a child. Back then, it always meant Lord Malmsby had pulled off a counter strategy to one of their mother's pranks. Aidan was delighted to see his brother hadn't totally forgotten his 'other' talents. And it looked like his sister Catherine agreed, for her eyes grew round and she raised a hand to her lips.

Candelstone looked around the table, his eyes landing on his wife. He must have had some inkling of concern by his wife's reaction. Candelstone's eyes narrowed. Aidan figured he'd just figured out he might have been checkmated.

"Spit it out, Malmsby," Candelstone said irritably.

"I also spoke to Lord Liverpool last evening."

"You're lying."

"Am I? He is not behind everything Lord Castlereagh does. Now that the war is over, he would like an opportunity to remove him from his position."

"You told him about the secret service?"

"No. Not yet, at least. I am a proponent of new technology and don't like what the radicals think is the solution, destroying the machines. I believe in education and new jobs, new kinds of jobs. But I dislike inviting men to skulk around to stir up trouble. That is your favored method of taking out the radicals. Encourage them to act so you can capture them when they do. Many would not act if not encouraged. They shout ideas and complaints to hear how they sound to their ears and the ears of others long before they decide to take action or not. And some never do."

"That's a naïve sentiment," growled Candelstone.

"Is it? It is ascribed to by Lord Liverpool, though."

Candelstone glared at him. "All right. I shall leave Lady Blessingame alone. I'll not pressure her to work for me. Bloody damn waste of talent, though."

"I'm afraid that is not good enough, now," said Malmsby, "now that I know the minds of Lord Liverpool and Lord Castlereagh."

"What do you mean?" Candelstone asked.

"Today, you will return to your townhouse to finish your recuperation. I have it on very good accord that they will offer you a secret diplomatic mission of your own. Out of the country. It should take you less than a year to complete. I am assured that by the time you return, a plan will be in place and an organization created to monitor and take care of radicals with no help from you."

"How dare you meddle in my work!" demanded Candelstone.

"I dare because I care. I care about the impact the new, upcoming technologies I admire will have on people. Some will be fearful and confused. We need to work with these fears and help people. We don't need to create more unemployed poor people in this country. That is not a way for our nation to grow and thrive."

"Thank you, and well said, Malmsby," Nowlton said. "But we have another matter to sort out. The shooter." Aidan turned to look at his sister. "Catherine, Candelstone said you figured out who the shooter was."

"Yes—well partly. Discussing it with William put the rest of the pieces together. I, too, believed Lady

Blessingame had killed the Spanish envoy. That is what William said. Believing he was dead made me hesitate," she explained apologetically, as she worried her fingers together.

"Catherine, would you like another cup of tea?" Malmsby asked her gently.

She turned to him, her features relaxing. She stuffed her hands into her lap. "Oh, yes, please, that would be wonderful."

Lord Malmsby signaled to the hovering footman, and the man brought the tea service over to Lady Candelstone.

"You know, your Bow Street Runner never interviewed me yesterday," she said chattily, nervousness gone as she busied her hands with making her tea. "I could have told him then I saw a man go into the Lady Margaret Parlor."

Aidan started to rise. Malmsby clamped his hand on his brother's wrist to force him to remain still.

"Why didn't you bring it up to him or to one of us?" Malmsby gently asked.

"I was so taken up with William," she said. "I was afraid to leave our rooms less he do something silly, like get out of bed."

Her husband frowned at her.

"Can you tell us now?" Malmsby asked.

"It was the Spaniard," she said.

"The Spaniard?"

"The musician who shared dinner with us last night."

"But that is Don Joaquín."

"I know that is who he *said* he is. He was in disguise, you know."

"Disguise?"

"He used blacking on his hair and wore a fake

mustache and goatee. Very good ones, they were, too. Top quality, not what one would typically see on stage."

"But you could tell they were fake?"

"Of course. I've made ones like that."

"I could use information about disguises in one of my books," said Lord Lakehurst, awed. "Might we talk more about disguises another day?"

"I'd be delighted to help an author," his aunt said, beaming at him.

She looked around the table. "Didn't any of you notice that when he blotted his brow last night at dinner that his handkerchief came away with black splotches?" she asked. "Blacking, not hair dye. He doesn't want to always wear this musician guise, so he doesn't have permanent hair dye. Still, he should have used something of better quality," Lady Catherine said, tutting.

"Seeing the black is why I asked Ellinbourne if I might go through his sketchbook. Once I saw the sketch and could study his features, I thought he must be a close relative of the Vizconde, and so I told William that night. That's when he told me the Vizconde was alive, and rumors in the spy world said he vowed revenge for being crippled."

"You bastard!" Aidan yelled, jumping out of his chair before his brother could grab him again. "You're dangling Bella like fish bait! Hoping he will come after her! I'll bet you suspected who shot you all along."

"He was a double agent! He cost many English lives. But we can't prove it to arrest him. So, we need to trap him into doing something we can arrest him for. That's why I need Lady Blessingame to work for me."

"No!" Aidan cried out in agony.

"Candelstone, get out!" Lord Malmsby ordered. "Both of you—out."

"You had better pray that no harm comes to Lady Blessingame for the game you have put into motion, or I will see you brought before judges for arranging a murder." Aidan swore to him.

"But Arthur—" whined Lady Catherine.

"Come along, Catherine," Candelstone ordered as he rose from the table. "They have no conception of what is due our *King and Country!*"

"I THOUGHT USING the traveling coach for a jaunt to Richmond to be ridiculous; however, it is a more comfortable ride compared to the town carriage," Gwinnie said as they left the tight, slow-going streets of the city for the road out to Richmond, and the coach moved on comfortably.

"Yes. I love this old thing," Lady Malmsby said. "I'd refurbish it before I'd replace it. You can't find springs like these in many carriages. Perhaps I should go ahead and have it refurbished before all the family weddings occur. You know I am looking at you, Gwinnie, to fall in line with your cousins and find a husband."

Gwinnie sighed. "We've gone over this multiple times, so all I'll say is don't get your hopes up. I'd look to Aidan and Lake before me."

"Aidan and Bella shall be next," Lady Malmsby said, expecting a reaction from Bella. "Bella," she said. She touched her leg.

Bella looked up. "Did you say something?"

"Yes, I did," said Lady Malmsby, "but what I said is

of no matter, it was me being a tease. You are wool-gathering. What are you thinking?"

"I am thinking of Ellinbourne's sketchbook," Bella said. She tilted her head, a faraway expression in her eyes.

"Ellinbourne's sketchbook? Why?" Lady Malmsby asked.

"Because last night Lady Candelstone suddenly developed an interest in looking through it."

Gwinnie looked puzzled. "Yes, but we all have looked at it and said how wonderful the sketches are," she said.

Bella nodded. "I watched as Lady Candelstone looked through it. She flipped quickly through one sketch after another. She didn't stop on any sketch until she came to the one of Don Joaquín, or who we *think* is Don Joaquín. "

"What do you mean?" Gwinnie asked.

"Haven't you ever noted his poorly died hair?"

"Of course, I have. Many men have vanity about their looks and growing older. I took it to be his vanity. It doesn't affect his musical ability."

Bella nodded. "After she put the book down—never looking at another sketch after she had come on that one—I picked up the book to look at that sketch again. Don Joaquín reminds me of someone, and has every time I've seen him. And it is a feeling of disquiet, almost fear that I get. He reminds me of a ghost."

"A ghost!" exclaimed Lady Malmsby. "What do you mean?"

"He reminds me of the Vizconde Miguel Carrasco-Torres."

"Who is that?"

"The man I shot in Brussels with a similar small pistol. I have been tormented for over a year with the memory of that night. I left not knowing if he was alive or dead. Yesterday, Lord Candelstone told me he was dead. But this musician, some of his mannerisms, his way of phrasing something, all remind me of the Vizconde."

"A relative?" Gwinnie suggested.

"I don't know, but I would say I was the intended victim and likely still am." She looked at both of them. "I am sorry. I should not burden you with this. I should not have allowed you to come with me! Since he heard us discuss the trip last night at dinner, I don't trust the Vizconde not to think our trip to Richmond is a splendid opportunity for revenge. We should have the coachman stop at the next inn or alehouse and allow you to stay there. It is not wise to be in my company.

"Well, *that* we won't be doing," declared Lady Malmsby. "It would be foolish of him to try anything while we are together."

"This makes little sense," Gwinnie protested. "You're reaching conclusions without facts. If this man wants revenge, why curry favor with me? I met him a month ago at the music publishers. I didn't know you, and only knew of you from three years ago when Uncle Aidan became a person I could no longer talk to as he fell into the darkest depression. We did not know you were coming to London or would stay with us."

Bella nodded. "Yes. The only people who knew I was coming to London were my brother and the lawyers." She scrunched her nose. "And if someone struck up a conversation with Andrew, I could see Andrew naively providing information about me, if he were asked."

"But that doesn't answer why befriend me and become a member of our ensemble," Gwinnie said.

"I disagree," said Lady Malmsby. "That is quite an astute move for a person who is a proficient musician, as this man obviously is. Musicians are needed for parties, balls, concerts, and musicales throughout the social season. If a person got with the right group of musicians, they would be able to eventually see Lady Blessingame, if she went to any entertainments. Once they found her, it would be a simple matter to discover her direction and whom she associates with, to discern what events she would attend," Lady Malmsby suggested.

"So, the only coincidence is Bella staying with us. His plan could work wherever she was," Gwinnie said.

"Yes. Music was the key to his access to her. He merely needed to be patient," Lady Malmsby said.

"And he didn't need to be patient for long, which was fortuitous for him," Bella said grimly. "I think he is Vizconde Miguel Carrasco-Torres. Lord Candelstone is wrong. He is *not* dead. If what we have discussed is true, he is a cunning man."

"Should we return to town then?" Gwinnie asked.

"Let's see how close we are to our destination," Lady Malmsby said. She rapped on the carriage hatch.

The hatch opened to the ruddy face of their coachman. "Yes, your grace?"

"How much farther to our destination?" she asked.

"We're almost there," the man said. "Another mile at most."

"Thank you. That is all," Lady Malmsby said.

"So, we go on," Bella said.

"We go on," Lady Malmsby concurred.

CHAPTER 13

RICHMOND

"Malmsby, how's your stable?" Aidan asked, after Lord and Lady Candelstone quit the breakfast parlor.

"I have Tintagel here. Not bloodstock, but muscular with excellent stamina. He could use stretching his legs. Jimmy," he said, turning his head to address the footman in the room. "Go see that Tintagel is saddled and ready for Aidan as soon as possible."

"Tell them to saddle my horse as well," said Lord Lakehurst.

"I assume you want to ride straight for Richmond?" Malmsby said.

"I do."

"I'll search out this Bow Street Runner of yours and let him know."

"Thank you." Aidan turned and left the room. His clothing was not riding attire; however, he would not go back to his townhouse to change. If they got ruined on the ride, so be it. He prayed the Vizconde would not use Bella's trip to Richmond as an opportunity to enact his revenge. But he couldn't trust he wouldn't.

Lake came rattling downstairs carrying an extra

riding crop and leather gloves. "These gloves will be better than your social gloves," he said, handing them to Aidan along with the riding crop.

The Duke came into the hall from the direction of his secretary's office. He carried two pistols. Aidan and Lake accepted the pistols. The footman opened the front door, and both men went outside. Not a word spoken. There was no need.

A groomsman came from the direction of the mews, riding a bay horse with a black mane and leading a large sorrel horse. The groom passed the reins of the sorrel horse to Lake and slid off the bay horse's back.

"Here you go, Mr. Nowlton. He's a mite fractious this morning, but he'll settle in soon enough," the groom said. He gave Aidan a leg up. The horse pranced and sidled at the unknown rider, but Aidan kept him in hand.

Aidan turned the horse toward the Richmond road and rode ahead, threading his way through the morning traffic. He silently damned every cart, carriage, horse, and pedestrian before him that forced him to keep the horse to a walk.

In his gut he felt the Vizconde would use Bella's, his mother's, and Gwinnie's trip to Richmond to his advantage. He would kill them all if he had to. Aidan could not let that happen. Would not let that happen.

And to think his brother-in-law was the author of the actions that set these events in motion was confounding. How his sister could be married to a man who could use people to achieve his goals, he could not fathom. And despite Candelstone's faith in Bella's abilities to protect herself, Aidan didn't trust the Vizconde. The man could use his mother and Gwinnie to get Bella to do as he wished. And Bella would do whatever the Vizconde asked in order to protect them.

He would not lose Bella again! He loved her more than he could have ever imagined. What a fool he'd been not to see through Harry. He knew what he was like; however, naively he thought Harry would never pull one of his stories on him. He was like a brother—no, he didn't know what a brother was like until today. Malmsby was always so many years older and caught up in the family's misusage of him.

Why had he let their *asks* continue? That was on him and no one else. He vowed the only *asks* he would jump to in the future would come from Bella.

The traffic thinned. Aidan and Lake flicked the tips of their crops to urge their horses on faster. Only ten miles away, he hoped they would catch up to the coach before they arrived.

～

"OH, this is quite lovely, my dear," said Lady Malmsby when the carriage pulled up before a tidy, white-washed, two-story building with an obviously new thatched roof. The groom handed them down before an open gate with a slate walkway leading to the front door.

"Please go to the nearest stable to tend to the horses and return in two hours," the Duchess told the man. Then she turned to Bella and Gwinnie. "Two hours should suffice, I think, don't you? We can go to the park to have our picnic, then return home."

"Yes, two hours should be ample for decorating discussions with Mr. Gladely," Bella said. "I wonder where he is? He said he would meet us here."

"Maybe he's inside," Gwinnie said as she looked

around. "Maybe I should look for my own establishment. I could see myself living in a place like this."

Her grandmother frowned at her. "Much too far from town and your music and your opportunity to make a parti."

Gwinnie laughed. "Give it up, Grandmother."

They walked toward the entrance porch. It had decorative woodwork scrolls painted a bright, light green, while the front door was a rich, dark green. The door was slightly ajar. "I think you are right, Gwinnie," Bella said as she pushed the door open. "Mr. Gladely!" she called out.

There was no response. They looked around. Someone tied a note to the newel post at the base of the stairs.

Come upstairs–JG

"He says to come upstairs, and those are his initials." Bella told Gwinnie and Lady Malmsby.

"But why hasn't he answered?" Lady Malmsby asked.

Bella shook her head and called again. "Mr. Gladely!"

After a moment, they heard a hoarse *"Here!"* followed by coughing.

"We are too easily spooked," Gwinnie said with a short laugh. She climbed the stairs followed by Lady Malmsby and Bella.

"Mr. Gladely where are you?" Bella called out as she got to the top of the stairs.

They heard a loud *thump, thump* from a room on the right, which was odd, for Bella thought the voice had come from the left. Empty houses had odd acoustics.

Gwinnie opened the door before Bella could stop her.

"Bella!" she yelled, as she rushed in.

Bella and Lady Malmsby followed swiftly.

They were in a small corner room with windows on two sides letting in bright sunlight in a broad swath across the floor.

In the bright beam lay a man bound hand and foot, with a gag in his mouth, his eyes wide and fearful.

The door slammed shut behind them, and with a *snick*, they heard the door lock.

Lady Malmsby grabbed the door handle. They were locked inside.

"Stupid, stupid," Bella said in disgust. "The oldest trick in the book and I fell for it." She dropped to her knees beside the man to loosen his gag.

"Mr. Gladely?" she asked.

"Yes," he managed to get out.

"I'm Lady Blessingame," she said, as she worked to pick apart the knots binding his wrists together. "And this is her grace, the Dowager Duchess of Malmsby, and her granddaughter, Lady Guinevere Nowlton," she told him tersely as she worked on the knots.

"Who did this?" she asked.

He shook his head. "Don't know. Foreigner," he said.

Bella and Gwinnie exchanged glances. "Spanish?" Bella asked.

"Maybe..." Mr. Gladely frowned. "Yes. Think he swore in Spanish."

"I thought he said he had a business appointment today," said Lady Malmsby.

"That's what he said," Gwinnie said. "Told me he came to England for business and had been neglecting his business for music. He had to do some work today."

"Any other way out of this room other than the door and windows?" she asked, as she pulled the last knot free.

"No," he said shakily. He pushed himself up to a seated position. Bella left him to untie his ankles.

"It's a steep drop out the windows," Gwinnie said as she stared out the window that was to the side of the house.

"I'm confident he doesn't mean for us to live," Bella said.

"You don't think he would go for a ransom?" asked Lady Malmsby.

"Maybe for you and Gwinnie, but not for me. He wants me dead."

"Beg pardon, my lady, but I did hear him say that," said Mr. Gladely shakily.

"It might be hard to separate us at this point," Gwinnie said.

"That is what I was thinking. Who's the lightest of us?" Bella asked.

"Grandmother," said Gwinnie.

"No, no," Lady Malmsby said. "I have old bones and bad joints. Even if you succeeded in lowering me down, I'd probably break something and be of no use. It will have to be Bella."

"What about me?" Mr. Gladely said.

Bella looked at him. "You are certainly on the small side, but no. I don't trust you," she said. She lifted her head and looked about. "Do you smell something?"

"Fire!" Mr. Gladely screamed. "He's going to burn us alive! He never said—"

"What Mr. Gladely. Said what? I thought you were in league with him when you drew our attention to this room with pounding your feet against the floor.

And Mr. Hargate said you were as honest as the day is long," she said disgustedly.

Bella lifted her skirts to take off her stockings. "Your cravat, Mr. Gladely, quickly."

Gwinnie and Lady Malmsby saw Bella's intention and removed their stockings as well. Bella tied them together along with Mr. Gladely's cravat. The entire length would not reach to the ground, but Bella reasoned it would get her far enough. She opened the window and sat on the ledge.

"Gwinnie, think you can hold me?" Bella asked.

"I honestly don't know, but you are our only hope, so I know I will. Promise of a Nowlton."

Bella nodded and eased herself out the window. The knots held, but she could see one slipping when she let go to drop the rest of the way to the ground.

She scrambled to her bare feet and ran back into the house. Smoke was billowing from the other end of the upstairs. Bella held her skirt up before her face as she made her way back upstairs.

The key was not in the lock. She could not open the door! "I can't open it" Bella called out with frustration and rage as she threw herself against the door. Nothing.

Suddenly, the door rattled from the other side as Gwinnie did the same on her side.

"There is a set of andirons downstairs by the fireplace," Bella yelled through the door. "I'm going to get one to see if I can break this thing."

"I'll keep trying from this side," Gwinnie yelled back as she threw herself at the door again.

Bella ran downstairs to grab up the iron rod. She would not let anyone die up there! That Spaniard would not win!

She could hear the crackling of the fire now. The other end of the house was ablaze.

She brought the iron down on the door lock. It seemed to loosen but not yet give. She raised the iron rod again.

It ripped out of her grasp. She screamed and turned to fight. It was Aidan! He pulled her out of the way as Lord Lakehurst ran at the door with his shoulder. The lock and the door shuddered and gave way, throwing Gwinnie to the floor on the other side.

Mr. Gladely ran out of the room as Lake and Aidan rushed in. Lady Malmsby was coughing from the smoke, gasping for air. Lake picked up his grandmother and rushed her down the stairs and outside. Aidan helped Gwinnie get to her feet. She'd hurt her ankle and foot when Lake crashed the door in, the weight of the door landing on her foot.

They heard the crash of a large beam somewhere in the fire.

"Get out of here!" Aidan yelled at Bella as he helped Gwinnie hobble forward.

Bella ran down the stairs and outside to where Lady Malmsby and Lake were.

"Go help them!" she yelled at Lake. "Gwinnie's hurt!"

The large man stormed back into the burning building. They heard another loud crash.

Out on the road, the fire brigade had arrived, passing buckets of water to wet down the thatch of the closest house, not even trying to save Bella's house.

Tears streamed down Bella's face. She clenched the Duchess's hand in hers. Finally she saw Lake come out of the house carrying Gwinnie, Aidan was behind him, his coat singed, his right arm hanging limply. In his left hand he held the iron rod.

The Malmsby crested coach came around the corner, the coachman doubtless drawn by the flames.

"No!" screamed a voice. It was the Spaniard running around the side of the house straight at Bella, a
gun in his hand. "You must die!" He took aim. Bella
saw a flash of movement, an iron rod slamming down
on his gun arm.

The Spaniard screamed in pain as the gun
dropped to the ground.

Aidan stumbled as the strike put him off balance
and, with his injured right arm, he couldn't catch himself. He fell, the Spaniard charging him. A shot rang
out and Vizconde Miguel Carrasco-Torres jerked, then
folded to the ground.

The Duke of Malmsby lowered his gun.

Bella ran to Aidan. He lay on the ground two feet
from the Vizconde's body. His hair singed, part of his
jacket burned away, and little burns from flying embers blackened one side of his face.

He flinched when she touched him. "My arm is
broken," he said, his voice smoke raspy. He coughed.

"If I help you, can you stand?" she asked, tears
streaming down her face.

"I'll get him up," Lord Lakehurst said. "Stand
aside, Lady Blessingame."

He grabbed Aidan under his arms and lifted him
up, staggering a bit. The Duke of Malmsby came up to
help steady them both. Bella saw Lord Lakehurst's
clothing had multiple burn holes and slight burns on
his hands and face.

Behind them, the burning roof and timbers of the
house crashed down in an explosion.

The locals backed away. One man approached
them. He bowed and pulled his forelock. "Everyone
make it out?"

"I—I think so," said Bella. "Mr. Gladely went out before us, but I don't see him about," she said, looking around.

"Gray-haired, spindly shanks bloke?" the man asked.

Bella laughed weakly. "That would describe him."

"Saw him scampering down the road. Probably in the alehouse by now."

"Farther, if he knows what's good for him," Bella said grimly. She looked at everyone, assessing their condition.

The Duchess's breathing appeared improved, but still hard. They needed to get her away from the smoke. After conferring with his father, Lord Lakehurst picked up his grandmother and carried her to the Malmsby coach.

The Duke examined Gwinnie's ankle, then helped her to stand, supporting her as she hopped toward the coach. Aidan hobbled toward Bella. She put her arm around him and together they made their slow way to join the others.

Mr. Martin rode up on a raw-boned horse. He jumped down and walked over to the Vizconde's body. He checked to ensure he was dead, then searched his pockets for any other identification or documents. When he straightened, he conferred with the local who'd approached them and appeared to be the leader of the fire brigade. Then he joined the rest of them clustered around the coach. The groom had dug out the picnic supplies and the Duchess was gratefully drinking water.

"What happened in there?" Bella asked Aidan.

"Unfortunately, I could not carry Gwinnie. I was trying to coax her down the stairs. A piece of wood cracked above us. I tried to shield Gwinnie and put up my arm to ward the falling wood away. That worked, but it broke my arm."

"And you caught on fire!" she said.

"A little, but Lake came up and kicked the wood away, slapped at my clothing to put out the fire, then picked up Gwinnie because he is big enough to carry her. It was but a moment. I'm amazed at my head-in-the-clouds writer nephew."

"Well, you shouldn't be. You have a capable family. Let them be capable," she said. She looked at his arm dangling. "That can't be good, for a broken arm to be hanging down like that. I'm going to remove your neckcloth and try to create a sling to support that arm," she said, and fussed with the cravat knot.

He lifted his chin to give her more access. "How did you end up escaping with the others still locked in that room?"

"We took our stockings off, tied them together along with Mr. Gladely's neckcloth. With our makeshift rope, Gwinnie held one end while I climbed out the window and down the side of the house." She pulled his neckcloth loose. "This will probably hurt for me to pull your arm up and tie the cloth around your neck."

"Let me help," said a voice behind her. It was Lord Malmsby. "I'll hold his arm up while you tie the cloth. Grit your teeth Aidan, this will hurt," he said, as he and Bella positioned his arm into a sling.

Aidan leaned against a coach wheel when the sling was secured. "How did you come to be here?" he asked his brother, his voice raw.

He nodded toward the Bow Street Runner. "Mr. Martin came shortly after you left. He'd interviewed Reggie Stafford. The lad said he saw the flutist come out of the room on the left, the one he thought was closed. After the shot was fired."

"The Lady Margaret Parlor," Aidan said.

His brother nodded.

"Why didn't he say anything that night?"

"Didn't connect him to the shot."

"Bloody Hell."

The Duke nodded. "I decided it was highly probable that the Vizconde would try to attack her here, out of London. I had Gwinnie's horse saddled and came on as fast as I could, leaving Mr. Martin to find his own mount."

"And got here just in time."

Lord Malmsby shrugged. "A duke has to have his uses," he said.

Aidan laughed weakly. He straightened. "We have to get the women home, I'll—"

"Stop," said Lord Malmsby, holding up his hand. "The Duke isn't done yet," he said, winking at Bella. "Aidan, you'll ride in the coach with the women. I'll ride Tintagel back and let Mr. Martin ride Gwinnie's horse. We'll tie that bone-shaker brute he rode here on to the back of the coach. Lake, how are you doing? Can you ride ahead to warn Merlin he has patients coming?"

Lake grinned, "Yes, your grace," he said, bowing stiffly. Lord Malmsby grinned back at him and cuffed him gently on the head. "On your way, then."

Lake mounted his horse and turned back toward the city as Lord Malmsby organized the others.

Aidan and Bella sat together on the rear-facing seat. He kept her close to him, not caring it was his mother and niece who sat across from him. He would not let Bella escape again. He sighed deeply. Ultimately, no one was seriously hurt, and—to his amazement—they had all worked together. Though Bella's house was a total loss, it could be rebuilt, but if he had any say in the matter, she would never live there. Richmond was too far from his gallery.

Aidan felt the happiest he had in years. An enormous weight had fallen off of him, and all because of Bella, the wonderful woman at his side. He smiled down at her.

"When are you two going to get married?" Lady Malmsby asked in a raspy voice, raspy now for the emotions that clogged her throat.

"As soon as I can get a special license," Aidan declared.

"What?" said Bella. "But you haven't even asked me yet, nor have I answered," she said playfully.

"Special license!" objected his mother.

"Yes, I'm not willing to let anything, anyone, or any time come between us again! Bella, love of my life, will you marry me? And remember, we now have witnesses," he said with mock sternness, nodding at his mother and niece.

"In a heartbeat," declared Bella, "for my heart has been yours for three years."

Aidan turned to kiss her.

Across from them, Gwinnie and the Duchess sniffed as tears slid down their cheeks.

EPILOGUE
FOUR MONTHS LATER

"Will that be all, Mrs. Nowlton?" asked the maid who'd brought her tea and scones.

"Yes, thank you, Beatrice," said Bella. She eyed the scones with delight. Food no longer made her stomach queasy, and she loved Cook's scones. She took a bite of one before pouring her tea. She closed her eyes as she savored the flavor. Not too sweet, with a lovely blend of spice.

"Ah, good, I came up before you could devour all the scones," said Aidan from the library doorway.

Bella's eyes flew open, and she quickly stood up and threw her arms around her husband, scattering crumbs across both of them.

"You know, my love, I would rather *eat* a scone than wear one," he teased.

"Yes, yes. But I am delighted you could join me today! You haven't in so long," she complained.

"I am delighted as well," he said, urging her to sit back down. He took a seat next to her. "Delighted to spend time with you, my wonderful wife and mother-soon-to-be, and delighted that the new gallery assistant is working out well. With a full staff, I believe I will feel comfortable leaving the gallery when we go to Versely Park for Ann's wedding to Ellinbourne."

"See, Gwinnie and I told you Miss Brinkley would be an excellent addition for the gallery. How are Mr. Tourmet and Mr. Coombs getting along with her?" she asked as she poured tea for him.

"Surprisingly well. And I didn't have to threaten them too much," he said.

"Aidan!" protested Bella.

"I'm teasing," he said.

She smiled. "It's nice to see you tease. Lord Candelstone could not call you a prig now! Speaking of Candelstone—"

"Must we?" Aidan asked tiredly. "He's far away in the West Indies."

"Yes, but his wife isn't. I saw Catherine today when I was at the Earl of Soothcoor's boys' orphanage. She is organizing the boys there for a Christmas Pageant. Costumes, wigs, makeup, everything. She is no longer moping and missing Lord Candelstone."

"Good, I hope she continues working with the charity children for plays and pantomimes when Candelstone returns, which hopefully won't be until late Spring at the earliest."

Aidan put his arm around her, and she leaned back into him as she sipped her tea. "I feel sorry for Ann having to wait so long before she and Ellinbourne can marry."

"If all goes well, his eldest sister will be back in England from Boston in the next couple weeks," Aidan said.

"I look forward to meeting her," Bella said. "Ann said she's been a governess in Boston for the last four years, long before anyone imagined Miles Wingate, a clergyman's son, would become the Duke of Ellinbourne." She picked up another scone.

"*If* she comes back to England. Ellinbourne says she has a broad streak of independence and wasn't happy when he became the Duke."

"Really? Well, sounds like there is a story there," Bella mused.

"Probably; however, at the moment, rather than thinking about other people," Aidan said, taking her teacup out of her hand and setting it back on the tray, "how about thinking of your husband." He pulled her across his lap.

"Oho, my favorite subject," she murmured, reaching up to run her hand through his hair as his lips came down to meet hers.

She closed her eyes and surrendered to his encompassing love.

THE END

SCRIBBLINGS BY HOLLY NEWMAN

The Art of Love
An Artful Deceit
An Artful Compromise
An Artful Lie

Flowers and Thorns *Series*
A Grand Gesture
A Heart in Jeopardy
Heart's Companion
Honor's Players

A Chance *Inquiry series*
The Waylaid Heart
Rarer Than Gold
Heart of a Tiger

Other *works*
Gentleman's Trade
Reckless Hearts
A Lady Follows
The Rocking Horse (novella)
Perchance to Dream (short story)

ABOUT THE AUTHOR

I decided to be a writer when I was in the fifth grade. I filled notebooks with stories—until a mean-spirited high school teacher told me I had no talent for writing. Crushed, for several years I stopped writing, but writing was an itch that wouldn't go away.

My interest in the Regency period came while in high school when I volunteered to re-shelve returned books at the community library. Every week there were Georgette Heyer novels to be shelved. I finally checked one out and became immersed in the world of the Regency.

Fast forward ten years. When attending Science Fiction Conventions, I met people who read science fiction, but also enjoyed the works of Jane Austen and Georgette Heyer, just as I did! They liked these books so much that they wore Regency costumes at the science fiction conventions. They even had Regency era dancing on the convention program. These science fiction readers and writers knew a lot about the Regency era. Intrigued, I did research on the era and quickly went from casual Regency reader to a Regency history buff. Woo-hoo!

After that, with encouragement from science fiction authors, it was just a small step to writing Regencies.

After living thirty years in the Arizona desert, I now live in Florida, seven miles from the Gulf Coast, with my husband, Ken, and our six cats.

Subscribe to my newsletter to learn about books and
other writings I'm working on. You can sign up here.
Or visit my website